DAN FREEDMAN

SCHOLASTIC

First published in the UK in 2010 by Scholastic Children's Books
An imprint of Scholastic Ltd
Euston House, 24 Eversholt Street
London, NW1 1DB, UK
Registered office: Westfield Road, Southam, Warwickshire, CV47 0RA

This edition published by Scholastic Ltd, 2012

ISBN 978 1407 13058 3

A CIP catalogue record for this book is available from the British Library.

Printed and bound by CPI Group (UK) Ltd, Croydon, CR0 4YY
Papers used by Scholastic Children's Books are made from wood grown in sustainable forests.

12

www.scholastic.co.uk/zone

Acknowledgements

Thanks to:

The Erlicks and Freedmans – for your support and for giving me a place to write!

Caspian Dennis, Ena McNamara, Lola Cashman, Martin Hitchcock, Oli Karger and Major – for your fantastic advice.

Hazel Ruscoe – this story is inspired by the ideas we had together.

The best left-winger of them all, Ryan Giggs – for backing Jamie.

Ms Pluckrose and the secret agents at St Ed's – for telling me exactly what you thought!

Jason Cox – for bearing with me on the double drag-backs!

Sarah Stewart and the whole team at Scholastic – for signing Jamie up.

And everyone who follows Jamie's story. He plays for you. . .

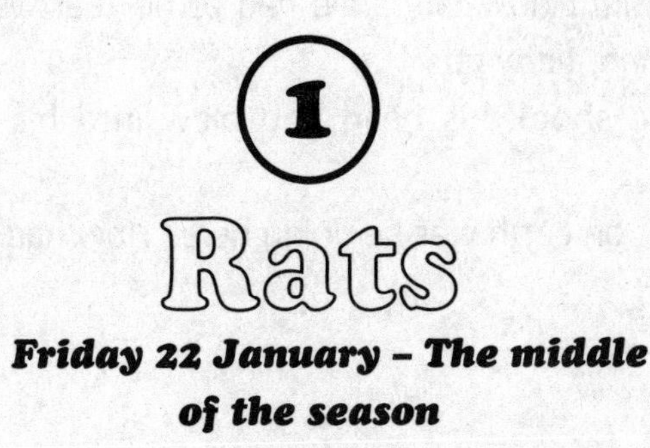

1 Rats

Friday 22 January – The middle of the season

Jamie was sure he could hear rats scurrying beneath the wooden floorboards of the manager's office at Seaport Town Football Club.

Rats, with their hairy little feet and their big sharp yellow teeth. Rats, crawling around with their noses twitching.

Jamie Johnson was in the third division of English football and he was sharing a football club with rats.

It was Jamie's first day at Seaport Town and he was waiting to meet his new manager, Raymond Porlock.

All Jamie wanted was to get back. Back to Hawkstone United . . . back to the Premier League . . . back to where he belonged. . .

Just a few months ago he had been a star. He'd been football's golden boy, with the world at his feet.

But, right now, all Jamie had at his feet were those disgusting, filthy rats. . .

Jamie shook his head and blew into his freezing hands.

What on earth was he doing here? How had he fallen so far?

Rewind – four months earlier

The beginning of the season

2 Top of the League

Saturday 12 September
Hawkstone United v Aldwich City
Live commentary from the Premier League. . .

"And Jamie Johnson has burst completely clear of the City defence once more. . . His speed is sensational! There's no way the defenders will catch him now!

"Just the goalkeeper to beat. . . This for Johnson's sixth goal in five games. . . This to send Hawkstone United to the top of the Premier Leaaaaaaague!

"Oh and it's there! Johnson knocked it in through the keeper's legs! That's the cheekiest goal you are likely to see! And another quite sensational strike from the boy with the golden touch!"

Premier League Table – 12 September

Team	P	GD	Points
1. Hawkstone United	5	+11	13
2. Aldwich City	5	+7	11
3. Larchester Rangers	5	+6	10
4. Crayhall	5	+2	9
5. Foxborough	4	+7	7
6. Brockburn Rovers	5	+6	7

Top Scorers – Race for the Golden Boot

Johnson	6
Rodinaldo	5
O'Kane	5
Afikware	4
Volpone	4
Rouzel	3

It was a boiling September afternoon. Hawkstone United were top of the Premier League and Jamie Johnson was fast becoming recognized as the best young player in the country.

Nothing could touch him. This was where he'd dreamed of being his entire life.

*

"Put the radio on, will you, Doug?" Jamie asked, as his driver pulled out of the Hawkstone car park.

Jamie had listened to the match reports on the radio since he was a young kid. He and his granddad, Mike, had always gone to watch the Hawkstone games together and then given each player marks out of ten on their way back.

Then, when they'd got home, they would switch on the radio to see what the pundits thought.

The only difference now was that Jamie was the player they were talking about on the radio. . .

"I'm pleased to say that we're now joined by the manager of Hawkstone United, Harry Armstrong," said the radio presenter.

"So, Harry, you may be the youngest manager in the Premier League, having just hung up your own boots, but with thirteen points from five games, the league table must make pretty good reading for you tonight.

"And we have to ask you about Jamie Johnson! He's still only seventeen years old, but right now he looks like the most potent attacker in the league. How good do you think this boy can become? Is it too early to start using the words 'world class'?"

"Well, Pat, every team needs someone to unlock the door. . . to provide that spark. At the moment, Jamie

Johnson is that person. He's a special player for us.

"And people shouldn't forget that it was only a year ago that he was injured so badly that it looked like the boy might not ever play again. Foxborough released him and he came to us. You know that his first job here was washing the kits?

"My assistant, Archie Fairclough, he has this saying: 'Never bet against Jamie Johnson,' and I'm starting to agree with him."

Jamie smiled, leaned back and looked out of the window. It was true. A year ago, he could hardly walk, let alone sprint away from Premier League defenders like an Olympic athlete.

Now, when defenders faced up to Jamie flying at them with the ball at his feet, he could see the fear in their eyes. And he loved that feeling.

Most of all, though, Jamie loved the fact that Harry Armstrong had called him a "special" player. That filled him with confidence. Made him feel unstoppable.

3
Jack's Back!

That weekend, Jamie Johnson and Jack Marshall were sitting in Sunningdale Park talking about football. It was the same as always. They had been coming here together for ten years, since they were kids at school, causing mischief together.

They were still just as close as they had ever been. Jamie didn't trust many people. He'd been let down too many times in the past, so now he didn't let many people get close to him.

Since Jamie's grandfather, Mike, had died, Jack was probably the only person in the whole world that Jamie properly opened up to. She was the one he would talk to if he had a problem or needed help.

He knew that he could trust her. He knew that Jack

would never let him down.

"Come on, JJ," Jack teased. "Give me some juicy Premier League gossip, then! What's the transfer news?"

Although Jack was studying for her A levels at college, she already knew that she wanted to be a football journalist. "That way, I'll get to go to all the best football for free!" she'd explained to Jamie. And, never one to hang around, she'd immediately got herself a part-time job working at the local newspaper.

"No way!" laughed Jamie. "I can't just tell you secrets and stuff!"

"Course you can! One bit of gossip from inside the Hawkstone dressing room; that's all I need," she said, her big brown eyes fixed on Jamie. "Go on! Tell me! Which players don't like each other? There must be some that hate each other's guts!

"Come on, Jamie!" she teased, tickling him now, in his weak spot, just below the ribs. "If I can get a good story, then the paper will give me a full-time job after my A levels! And that'll mean I can write loads of articles saying what a wicked footballer you are! See? Everyone's a winner!"

"Get off!" said Jamie, trying to stop Jack's tickling.

"All sounds great, Jack, except for the fact that . . . I can't tell you anything. I tell you, then it goes in the paper . . . and on the radio . . . and on the TV . . . and on the Internet . . . and then the whole world knows! What happens in the dressing room stays in the dressing room. That's what everyone says. It's like some golden rule in football. If I start blabbing, telling secrets and stuff, everyone'll hate me."

"Yeah, fair enough," said Jack, kicking the grass underneath the bench. "Wouldn't want to put you in a difficult position. And don't worry, I'll get my story in the end. You know what I'm like when I put my mind to something."

"Yeah, I know that all right," smiled Jamie, thinking back to the countless arguments he'd lost to Jack over the years. You could see it in her eyes: a sparkle . . . a fight. Jack was a winner. Perhaps that was why Jamie liked her.

Looking at her, Jamie reckoned that Jack was one of those people who could have been anything they wanted in life. She was good enough to be a top goalkeeper and pretty enough to be a catwalk model.

On the other hand, Jamie knew that *he'd* only ever had one option for what he could be – a footballer. So it was lucky that he just happened to be one of the best footballers in the country.

"Cheers for understanding it from my side," said Jamie. "I know that I'm lucky to have you as my—"

"Oh no!" Jack snapped, before Jamie could finish. "You're not going to start getting mushy on me, are you? Don't even go there! You're an idiot sometimes, Jamie Johnson!

"And anyway," she said, suddenly getting up off the bench and running out of the park, "if you want some of that chicken that my mum made for you, you better get your skates on – otherwise I'm having it all!"

Jamie leapt on to his feet and into a turbo-charged sprint. That was his favourite dinner!

4 Nemesis

Saturday 17 October

Premier League Table

Team	P	GD	Points
1. Hawkstone United	8	+13	18
2. Foxborough	7	+14	16

KICK-OFF 3 P.M. TODAY

It was the morning of the top of the table match against Foxborough.

Not only were Foxborough the clear favourites for the Premier League – having only narrowly missed out last season – they were also Jamie's former club; the club that had rejected him when he'd got injured.

There was no team in the world that Jamie wanted to put one over on more than Foxborough.

Of course Foxborough knew by now that they had

made a catastrophic mistake in releasing Jamie. Right now, he was the hottest property in football. But that didn't stop him wanting to show Foxborough what they were missing every time he stepped out on to the field against them.

Jamie Johnson seemed to be the name on everyone's lips at the moment. There were even massive posters of him plastered all over the local area.

Jamie had been paid handsomely to sign up to be the new face of a big sportswear company – he'd had the photo shoot last week. He'd practised his smile in front of the mirror for ages before the shoot but then, when he'd got there, they had asked him to scowl at the camera instead of smile.

They had told him to suck in his cheeks and look as "mean and moody" as he could. Now, as Jamie arrived at the Hawkstone stadium for the biggest match of the season so far, he could see why.

Outside the ground there was a giant poster of Jamie, staring straight down the camera, holding a gleaming new pair of boots in his hands.

Below were the words:

Some people say football is a matter of life and death.
But I know it's far more important than that...
Nemesis, The Ultimate Football Boot,
as worn by Jamie Johnson.

The cheer when Jamie got out of the car at the Hawkstone stadium was as loud as that which greeted any goal. The Hawkstone fans loved Jamie more than any other player. Because he'd grown up and gone to school in the area, most of the fans either knew him or pretended they did.

And they loved the fact that he hadn't moved either; he still lived in the same house on the same estate that he'd grown up in. Even though he'd soon have enough money to buy a massive pad on the other side of town, Jamie had agreed to stay at home with his mum and his stepdad, Jeremy, and put his money into a special account that he could only access when he was twenty-one.

He'd seen with his injury last year how quickly the whole Premier League dream could evaporate. Besides, this way he still got all his washing and ironing done!

Jamie signed as many autographs as he could but, after ten minutes, he went into the players' entrance to get ready for the game. He knew that even if he stayed outside signing for the next two days, he *still* wouldn't get them all done.

As soon as Jamie walked into the dressing room, he picked up the newspaper and scanned the back pages. Perhaps he should never have picked up the paper. Perhaps he should have just gone straight on to the pitch and started warming up.

But Jamie always read the newspaper before the game. It was as much a part of his pre-match ritual as putting on his boots.

But when he saw that day's headline, he stopped dead in his tracks.

4

The Mercury, Saturday 17 October

SPORTS NEWS

"JOHNSON DOESN'T CARE ABOUT ME"

Exclusive By Barry Digmore

Soccer star's dad reveals his heartbreak at being "dumped" by son

Jamie Johnson, the young teenage superstar currently taking the football world by storm, has not spoken to his own father for **FIVE MONTHS,** this newspaper can exclusively reveal. In a heart-wrenching interview, Johnson's father, Ian Reacher, reveals his family hell for the first time:

- **Johnson ignores father's phone calls**
- **Johnson has not given any money from his bumper new contract to his near penniless dad**
- **Star even changed his surname from Reacher to his mum's maiden name of Johnson**

"I can't believe the way he's turned his back on me," says Reacher, 38. "He was still just playing for his school team a few years ago. But I knew he had the talent and I believed in him. I was the one who got him his first contract in professional football.

"But now he's a Premier League star, he doesn't want to know me. People are going on about what a great footballer he is but I think it's time that people knew the truth about him as a person."

DIGMORE'S DIG: Yet another example of a footballer getting too big for his boots! You should always remember who put you on top because they can bring you down again just as quickly.

Are you related to a famous footballer? Got a story to tell? Email BARRY at digthedirt@digmore.com and earn yourself some cash!

6 Foxes on the Hunt

Hawkstone United 0 - 0 Foxborough
24 MINS PLAYED

The match had kicked off twenty minutes ago. One of the biggest matches of the whole season. A face-off between the top two clubs in the league. And all Jamie could think about was that stupid article in the newspaper.

It just continued to swirl around his mind. He tried to stop it. Tried to calm the hurt and anger inside him, but it was too strong. It was consuming him.

Just a pack of lies! None of what he said is true! I never abandoned him. He's the one who abandoned me!

And if I ever get my hands on that Barry Digmore, I'll—

CRUNCH!!

Jamie had held on to the ball too long. Instead of picking a quick pass or motoring down the wing, he'd dallied in possession, giving the Foxborough centre-half – a hairy brute of a man – just enough time to nail Jamie with a bone-crunching tackle.

Jamie lay on the ground for a second or two, half-heartedly appealing for a free-kick, but the referee had already waved play on. Jamie slowly picked himself up off the turf. He was a million miles off the pace.

Hawkstone United 0 - 0 Foxborough
65 MINS PLAYED

Glenn Richardson, Hawkstone's ultra-skilful playmaker, had used his trickery on the edge of the area to win Hawkstone a free-kick. It was perfectly positioned, twenty yards from goal, just to the right of centre. A great chance for Hawkstone to fire the opening goal.

Jamie had already scored two sumptuous free-kicks from this spot this season. One of them – which had smashed against the underside of the crossbar, hit the ground and then bounced back up into the roof of the net – had even won goal of the month in August. Millions of people had voted for it. Jamie kept the trophy above his bed at home. Sometimes he kissed it before he went to sleep!

Jamie gathered in a huddle with three other Hawkstone players to discuss what they were going to do with the set-piece. They covered their mouths so that the defenders couldn't hear what they were planning.

But Jamie's mind was drifting elsewhere. . .

It was going back to all the nights that Jamie had spent wishing, hoping that his dad would come back home, that they could all be just like a normal family again.

And when his dad *had* got back in touch last year, Jamie had been the happiest person in the world. His dad had even helped him to sign for Foxborough. Everything had been perfect. Until Jamie got injured.

Injured so badly that Foxborough said they had to let him go. Injured so badly it looked as though he would never play football again. . . And was Jamie's dad there for him when Jamie really needed him? Did his dad say everything was going to be OK and that he would be right behind Jamie, no matter what?

No. His dad had disappeared. Again. He'd just left Jamie lying there in the hospital bed. He didn't even bother calling to see if Jamie was going to be al—

"What do you think, Jamie?" Glenn Richardson was asking him. He was speaking out of the side of his mouth like a ventriloquist.

"Er . . . yeah, mate. . ." said Jamie, vacantly.

There was no way he could tell them that he had missed the entire conversation about what they were going to do.

So it came as a something of a relief to Jamie when Glenn Richardson himself took three steps back, deliberately marking out his run up to take the free-kick.

Good, Jamie thought. *They've decided to let Glenn take it. I don't feel like taking this one anyway*.

Jamie watched Richardson sprint up to the ball. *Go around the wall! There's a gap to the side of the wall!* Jamie urged his teammate.

Glenn Richardson arched his body and drew his foot back and then . . . he dragged the ball backwards . . . towards Jamie. . .

That was it! The plan wasn't for Richardson to take on the shot, it was for him to fake the shot, fool the keeper and for Jamie to have a go from a different angle.

Now all eyes were on him as he raced towards the ball. He had to get there before the defenders, who had already broken out from the wall to charge down the shot.

Jamie got there first. Just.

He swiped his boot at the ball with all the power in his body.

But no accuracy. He didn't even look at the ball properly as he unleashed his strike.

He was in such a rush to get in his shot that he had forgotten completely about his free-kick technique – *keep your head over the ball, keep your body compact . . . and above all . . . keep your composure. . .*

Jamie knew the words off by heart. His granddad, Mike, had drummed them into him since the day he'd first kicked a ball.

But Jamie wasn't in touch with his either his body or his mind. His foot slashed wildly at the ball.

The contact was awful. His toe only poked the side of the ball, sending it not curling handsomely towards the top corner but spinning crazily along the ground . . . to the touchline.

In the end, Jamie's shot went out for a throw-in to Foxborough. A throw-in! He hadn't even managed to get the ball to go as far as the goal! How pathetic! Jamie could not have been more disgusted with himself.

As the fans of both sides jeered his effort, Jamie put his head in his hands and, for a moment, dropped to his knees.

If he could, he would have dug a hole in the ground and disappeared.

FULL-TIME
Hawkstone United 0 - 2 Foxborough
M Whittle, 73
E Afikware, 84

SPORTS NEWS

Hawks knocked off their perch!

Foxborough snatch top spot!

Has Johnson lost his touch?

Premier League Table – 17 October

Teams	P	GD	Points
1. Foxborough	8	+16	19
2. Hawkstone United	9	+11	18
3. Larchester Rangers	9	+6	16
4. Crayhall	9	+4	15
5. Aldwich City	9	+7	15
6. Brockburn Rovers	9	+6	14

7 Breaking News

It wasn't long before everyone began to notice. Jamie was not the same player.

He'd lost something from his game. It wasn't as simple as his pace, or his control, or even his skill. It was something else that had disappeared. And it was impossible for Jamie to try to get it back because he didn't quite understand what it was . . . what he'd actually lost.

But it was obvious that defenders were simply no longer scared of him. The reputation that he had had previously – *the unstoppable Jamie Johnson . . . the winger with the sprinting speed of an*

Olympic champion . . . the attacker with the magic feet – had gone.

Now defenders were told to "get tight". To "put Johnson under pressure". "He'll crack . . . his confidence has gone."

Some of them had even started winding him up during games.

"You're not the real Jamie Johnson," one defender had said. "You can't be – you're rubbish! You egg!"

It became the norm for Harry Armstrong to substitute Jamie after sixty-five minutes, and pretty quickly, Jamie wasn't even that upset to see the subs board going up. In fact, he was relieved. He knew he was not showing the real Jamie Johnson out there. He was not doing himself justice.

The worst point came when, against Barnforth in the Cup, the Hawkstone fans actually cheered when Jamie was substituted.

That killed Jamie. This was the club he loved. The whole aim of his life was to play for Hawkstone and to be a hero with the Hawkstone fans. For them to cheer him going off – for them to want to get rid of him – cut him like a knife. He was just pleased that Mike had not been there to see it.

But even then. . . Even at that horrible moment, Jamie still had no idea what was coming next.

Wednesday 20 January

Jamie poured himself some cereal and turned on the TV as soon as he got in from training. As usual, nobody was around. His mum and Jeremy were spending a lot of time in Scotland these days.

It was where Mike had come from and, since he had died suddenly last year, going back there had been Jamie's mum's way of coping.

She had got really close to her family up there and had been up to visit three or four times. It didn't bring Mike back – nothing could – but spending time with her dad's family made Jamie's mum feel better. He could hear it in her voice when she called him.

Jamie was watching Sports News. He wanted to check the league table. Hawkstone had dropped points recently, and he was more to blame than most. Although they were still second, they were now three points behind Foxborough.

Jamie was analysing the goal-difference because, at the end of the season, it could be worth an extra point.

Premier League Table

Teams	P	GD	Points
1. Foxborough	17	+25	38
2. Hawkstone United	17	+22	35
3. Larchester Rangers	17	+16	33
4. Aldwich City	17	+17	31

He turned the sound on mute so he could just concentrate fully on the figures. It was as hard as a maths test at school!

And that was why it took a second for Jamie's eyes to flick to the breaking news at the bottom of the screen.

BREAKING NEWS ... HAWKSTONE ANNOUNCE SIGNING OF MATTHEUS BERTORELLI ... WORLD-FAMOUS LEFT-WINGER SIGNS FOR £13.8 MILLION ... BERTORELLI SIGNS FOUR-YEAR CONTRACT ... BERTORELLI BECOMES HAWKSTONE UNITED'S RECORD SIGNING ... SHOCK SWOOP STUNS FOOTBALL WORLD ... LIVE PRESS CONFERENCE IN HALF AN HOUR...

Jamie spat his entire mouthful of cereal halfway across the room.

8

Bertorelli's Pants

"Jack," said Jamie. "It's me. Can you talk?"

He'd called her immediately. He was panicking. He couldn't stop thinking that Hawkstone had signed Bertorelli to replace him. He needed Jack now. Needed her to talk some sense into him.

"Hi, Jamie! Yeah, I can talk for a sec. I'm at the ground. It's mental here! They're going crazy over this whole Bertorelli signing! They've even found some old pics he did advertising underpants!"

"Yeah, that's what I wanted to talk to you about." Jamie could hear loads of noise in the background.

"What? His pants?"

"No, stupid! Him signing. It's a disaster, isn't it?"

"Disaster? How? You're not jealous, are you, Jamie? You should be proud. Hawkstone signing Bertorelli shows that they're really ready to take on the big boys!"

"Yeah, but think about it, Jack. Where's he gonna play? He's a left-winger. He's here to replace me, isn't he?"

Jamie could feel his anxiety rising. He hated the idea of being dropped more than anything in the world.

"That depends, doesn't it?" said Jack. "Harry Armstrong will just pick his best eleven players – like any manager. . . Look, let's talk about this later. The press conference is about to start. You need to trust yourself, JJ."

Jamie stared at Mattheus Bertorelli on the TV and shook his head.

The man was wearing a pink shirt with about five buttons undone so everyone could see his bare chest, which, by the look of things, he'd had waxed! He was also wearing a necklace and an Alice band around his hair. He looked as though he'd come fresh from the catwalk, not a football pitch!

"You look like a girl, mate!" Jamie said out loud. He couldn't stop himself laughing. This guy was a joke!

"So why Hawkstone, then, Mattheus?" a journalist was asking as the press conference to announce Bertorelli's arrival kicked off. "You could have joined any club in the world – Milan, Madrid, Juventus, Barcelona – so what made you choose Hawkstone United?"

Hang on a minute! Jamie thought to himself. *I recognize that voice!* And sure enough, the camera turned to show that the journalist asking the question was Jack!

Jamie leapt up from the sofa. He couldn't believe she was on TV! And she'd sounded so professional!

Jamie looked at her face on the screen as she waited for her question to be translated.

She was dressed really smartly. She looked amazing! And she even had a proper media pass pinned to her shirt. Jamie noticed that it said Jacqueline Marshall rather than just "Jack". Did she want to be known as Jacqueline now, then? Jamie liked that name. . .

"I can answer you question in simple way," Bertorelli responded, running his fingers across his little goatee. "I am . . . how you say? Explorer in football. . . And to come to Hawkstone is new adventure for me.

"I here to give joy with my football . . . to make many new friends with my skill."

"And what about Jamie Johnson, Mattheus?" another journalist was asking now. "He plays the same position as you and is a big favourite with the fans. Do you think you might face a battle for that spot on the left wing or are you confident of winning a place in the starting line-up?"

"Soon the fans will love me," Bertorelli answered immediately. "I am a special player. I have been blessed with my talent. Maybe in the future, this boy you talk about – Jonny Jackson – maybe he can be a very good player too. But now, is maybe the best thing for him to try to learn from me."

Jamie picked up the remote control and threw it at the TV. Hard. The control smashed into the screen and the batteries went flying in different directions.

"What an absolute muppet!" Jamie snarled, kicking his own sofa in frustration. "Blessed with talent?! He'll be blessed with my left boot if he's not careful!"

9 Phoney!

Jamie didn't have to look up to know that Bertorelli had entered the dressing room. The thick waft of expensive aftershave announced his arrival clearly enough. His presence disgusted Jamie.

And to make matters worse, all the other players were crowding around Bertorelli as though he were the coolest kid in the playground.

Bertorelli was loving the attention too, telling his new teammates all the tricks he had picked up at his previous clubs.

"No! No! No!" He was laughing. Even his laugh sounded fake. "No, you must never give *all* the autographs! They only sell them on Internet anyway! No, you choose the ones you give autographs. Give to the ones you like. . . Only the pretty girls!"

The Hawkstone players cracked up, encouraging Bertorelli to further explain his off-the-field tactics.

"And same with interviews," he said, pointing his finger to illustrate his point. "No interviews . . . apart from with the beautiful ladies! Me? Maybe I give exclusive to the journalist who asked me first question! I remember her name: Jackie. Yeah, Jackie . . . she *very* pretty! I give her exclusive!"

Jamie, who was putting on his boots with his back turned to Bertorelli, was just about to explode with rage.

Thursday 21 January

The next morning, Jamie was in the Hawkstone training ground car park. Doug, the driver, had gone to get a cup of tea from the canteen while Jamie sat in the car finishing off some emails on his phone before he went into training. He heard tooting and saw Bertorelli driving his Ferrari up to the security barrier at the entrance to the car park. Most players stopped to sign autographs for the fans hanging around the security booth, but Bertorelli just drove right past them! He pulled up in the space next to Doug's car.

Jamie slouched down lower in his seat. He had no

desire to talk to Bertorelli.

Jamie had done some digging on Bertorelli on the Internet last night. He'd found out that, during his whole career, Bertorelli had never stayed at any club longer then two years.

He had always come in, been paid lots of money, won a trophy or two and then moved on for the next payday.

And that was what made no sense at all to Jamie: Hawkstone were not a rich club. They were a good club, with a great history, but they did not pay any of their players mega wages. So if Bertorelli hadn't come to Hawkstone for the money, why *was* he here? He had to be *using* Hawkstone for something. But what?

Through the open window, Jamie realized Bertorelli was on the phone – and he could hear exactly what Bertorelli was saying. Jamie felt his heart pounding. Maybe if he listened, he'd be able to find out what Bertorelli was really up to. . . It felt as though his whole career at Hawkstone might just depend on it.

However, the more he listened to Bertorelli's conversation, the more embarrassed Jamie was becoming.

"Yes," Bertorelli was saying. "I will do lots of work with the charities and I will visit all the local schools. It is very, very important that I do the good work outside of the football. There is nothing more important than this."

Jamie felt his cheeks flush with shame. He had misjudged Bertorelli badly. Here Jamie was spying on him and all Bertorelli was talking about was what he could do for the local community. Jack had been right, like always – it could only have been jealousy that had made Jamie suspicious of Hawkstone's new signing.

Jamie sent his last email and looked at the time on his phone. Training was starting in twenty minutes. It was time to let this vendetta against Bertorelli go. Time to get ready for training. . .

Jamie was just about to sit up and open the door when, through the wing mirror of Bertorelli's car, he saw Bertorelli look around him, checking to ensure that no one was there. There was a look in Bertorelli's eyes that seemed to say he was hiding something.

Instinct told Jamie to stay exactly where he was. He slouched back down into the seat.

"And the reason that I make myself act like this saint is that it means no one will suspect me!" said Bertorelli.

And then he started laughing. The sound alone made Jamie shudder.

Bertorelli was running his fingers through his hair now as he listened to the person on the other end of the phone.

"Of course I can make it happen, you fool!" Bertorelli whispered angrily. "I already have a plan. It is simple but genius. In a very big game, near end of the season, I can make sure I get a red card after five minutes . . . I do a bad foul and swear at the referee or something. Anyway, I am sent off after five minutes. And then we know for sure that Hawkstone will lose this game. It is one-hundred per cent they will lose because they have stupid players. Without me, they are nothing. They will lose badly.

"So, I tell you which game, you make the bets on Hawkstone to lose and you win your money. Lots of money. All the money I owe you and more. In *one* match. Like I say, is simple and genius."

Jamie felt his heart start to speed, start to hammer away inside his chest, while his brain attempted to decipher what exactly was going on.

"Yes, I know how much I owe you!" snapped Bertorelli. "Why do you think I join this rubbish club? I'm here to do this. Just wait. Let me make good reputation first so no one suspects and then I call you and tell you which game. . . Don't worry, I can do this. You will get your money! Now leave me alone!"

And then Bertorelli hung up the phone, looked around one final time, got out of his car and went into training.

Jamie watched him go and, as soon as Bertorelli was out of sight, he breathed in a massive gulp of air. He'd been holding his breath for ages.

He could not believe what he had just heard. Jamie thought Bertorelli might have been up to no good, but this – fixing matches – this was something else. . . And the feeling in Jamie's stomach told him that there was going to be some serious trouble ahead.

But there was no backing out of it. Jamie was a part of this now, whether he liked it or not.

He knew exactly what he had heard and, more importantly, he knew he had to do something about it.

10
Kicking Off!

"See, everyone?" Harry Armstrong was saying. "If we just give the ball to this guy, he can work magic for us. Do things that no one else can do. He is a special player."

Bertorelli had just bent a perfect free-kick right into the top corner of the goal and Harry Armstrong had stopped training for the third time to personally praise his new signing in front of everyone else.

It was becoming too much for Jamie. It was almost as though Harry was sucking up to Bertorelli. *Why don't you just go over and kiss the bloke if you think he's that amazing?* Jamie thought. *But you don't know what I know. You don't know the truth about him . . . why he's really here . . . what he's planning. . .*

"OK," said Armstrong, now strolling over to the kit bag and blowing his whistle hard and loud. "Gonna mix it up a bit now, bring a little competitive spirit into things. Full-size game, proper match tempo, and we're gonna have the youngies versus the oldies. Under twenty-fives in bibs that side, over twenty-fives that side. I want a hundred per cent but no crazy tackles . . . we've got a big game on Saturday."

It had been ninety minutes since Jamie had heard Bertorelli's phone call. Heard his plan. His plan to fix a game. His plan to cheat.

Every minute had seemed like a week, with sickness pumping through Jamie's body like poison as he tried to work out what he should do, who he should tell. . .

Now he was watching Bertorelli juggling the ball in the centre of the training pitch. Bertorelli was chewing gum, looking around him at the other Hawkstone players. It was so clear to Jamie now. So clear that Bertorelli thought he was better than anyone else here. He did not respect them. He did not respect football.

Even before the practice game kicked off, Jamie could feel his forehead glisten with a film of sweat. Tension raged within him. He had to do something to stop this traitor. . .

And then suddenly, as Bertorelli picked up the ball and started doing his fancy skills, the answer came to

Jamie in a flash. There *was* a way to stop Bertorelli; a way to prevent him from being able to carry out his plan. It was so simple Jamie couldn't believe that he hadn't worked it out earlier.

He had to take Bertorelli out!

Jamie did not like the idea of fouling another player on purpose – and he certainly would not have considered doing it to any other player – but for Bertorelli, for a cheat, he was prepared to make an exception.

Jamie turned and charged at Bertorelli.

He quickly built up to his top speed and then launched himself at Bertorelli with a flying, waist-high, kung-fu tackle. He gave him everything he had. He had to take Bertorelli out of the game for months . . . it was the only way. . .

But Bertorelli was too quick. He swerved out of the way before Jamie could make contact.

Jamie went flying through the air, studded boot outstretched, a look of pure aggression etched on his face. But he got nowhere near Bertorelli.

And now he had been exposed.

"Eh!!" Bertorelli shouted furiously, throwing his hands up into the air. "You crazy! What you do, little boy? You want to kill me, you idiot?!"

"I'm no idiot!" Jamie roared, springing up off the

ground and sprinting straight at Bertorelli. "I know what you're doing, you che—"

But before he could get the words out, before he could tell everyone what he'd found out, what was going on, he felt his legs and his body being lifted powerfully from the ground and marched off the pitch. He struggled but he couldn't release himself from the grip.

Both Harry Armstrong and Rigobert West, Hawkstone's titan of a centre-half – the man they called The Beast – had hold of Jamie and they would not let him go until he was far enough away from the other players not to be a threat.

"Get rid of him!" shouted Bertorelli as they dragged Jamie away. "I not play in same team as that idiot!"

"It's him!" Jamie screeched, pointing at Bertorelli, unable to control his voice and his emotions when they finally put him down. "We've got to stop him. You don't know what he's up to!"

"Go and wait for me in my office!" shouted Harry Armstrong, so angry a vein was bulging out from the side of his forehead.

"But Harry!" Jamie said. "You don't understand! It's Bertorelli! He's going to f—"

"Now, Jamie! Get in my office NNNNOOOWWW!"

11

Sent Down

Jamie sat in Harry Armstrong's office, waiting. His heart was still racing and his fists were still clenched. He wished he'd had the chance to give Bertorelli everything he deserved. He might not get another opportunity.

How could Bertorelli do it? How could he cheat football?

Jamie wouldn't allow him to. He couldn't stand by and watch this traitor use Hawkstone like this.

Hawkstone was the team that Jamie thought about when he went to sleep. It was the team that was written in his blood.

And that meant that he *had* to stop Mattheus Bertorelli.

Because he was the only person who could.

"I'm disappointed in you, Jamie," Harry Armstrong announced, sweeping into the room like a hurricane. "Seriously disappointed."

He was staring at Jamie now. His eyes were harsh and cold.

"I'm sorry, boss, but you don't understand . . . it's Bert—"

"I haven't finished yet," Armstrong barked. "The reason I'm so disappointed in you is that you're a Hawkstone fan. You're always going on about how you were a mascot here when you were eleven, about how proud you are to play for this club. You, of all people . . . I didn't expect you to react like this."

"React to what?" Jamie asked. "I don't understand."

How come he was the one who was in trouble when it was Bertorelli who was the cheat?

"React like this to us signing Bertorelli!" said Armstrong, his face reddening with anger. "Bertorelli is the single biggest signing this club, *your* club, has ever made.

"And how do you react? Like a spoilt child! Just because the guy plays in your position, from the minute he walks through the door, you go into a strop and start causing problems for the rest of the squad. I mean, what was that out there today? It was an absolute disgrace! That's what it was!"

"Boss," said Jamie, suddenly aware of the gravity of the situation facing him. "Boss, it's not like that. I haven't got a problem with Bertorelli because he plays left wing. It's . . . it's something else. . ."

"What is it then, Jamie? If it's money, then you can forget it; you've just signed a new contract. You're the highest-paid teenager in the country, for God's sake! There's no way you're getting another—"

"No," said Jamie. "It's not about money . . . well, not as far as I'm concerned, anyway. . ."

"What are you talking about, Jamie?' Armstrong demanded. "And let me tell you, this had better be good, because I'm rapidly losing patience."

"Bertorelli!" Jamie spluttered. "He's a . . . cheat! A fake! He's planning to throw a game! I heard him admit it on the phone this morning!"

Now he'd said it, Jamie felt the relief seep through his body. It was as though a huge pressure had been released. A burden lifted. Now Harry Armstrong knew the truth and he could deal with Bertorelli himself.

Jamie sensed Harry Armstrong's stare zoning in on him.

"Who's he working with?" asked Armstrong.

Jamie suddenly felt as though he were the one on trial.

"I don't know," said Jamie. "He didn't say."

"Which match is he planning to throw?"

"I don't know," stammered Jamie, searching his

mind for what he'd heard. "I think one at the end of the seas—"

"OK," said Harry Armstrong, with no trace of emotion in his voice. "I think I've heard just about enough. This is not what I wanted to do, Jamie, but the way I see it, I don't have any other choice."

And then, right there in front of Jamie, Harry Armstrong took out his phone and called his old friend Raymond Porlock – the manager of Seaport Town Football Club.

It was that quick. Before Jamie had a chance to say another word, he was out of Hawkstone United.

Jamie was told not to report to Hawkstone for training the next day but to head to Seaport Town instead. Tiny little Seaport Town. In the third tier of English football. It may only have been twenty miles from Hawkstone, but it was a football world away.

"A three-month loan period," Harry Armstrong had explained on Hawkstone's website. "To allow Jamie to rediscover his form and confidence away from the pressure of the Premier League. It's the best thing for him right now. He'll come back to us a better player."

But Jamie knew the truth. Jamie knew that he'd been shipped out of his club because the manager thought that he held a grudge against the star player. Because the manager thought he was there to cause trouble.

And most haunting of all were Armstrong's last words as he practically shoved Jamie out of his office:

"If you so much as breathe a word of this to anyone – and I mean *anyone* – if you undermine the best season that this club has *ever* had, I swear, Jamie, I'll see to it that you never play for Hawkstone United again."

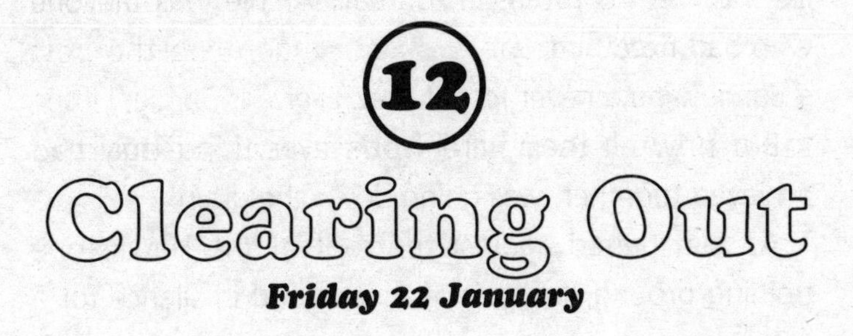

12 Clearing Out

Friday 22 January

"Don't worry, I'll make sure it's still there when you get back," said a familiar voice as Jamie cleared out his locker the next morning.

It was 7.30 a.m. He was supposed to be at Seaport Town at 9.30 to meet their manager, Raymond Porlock, in his office.

Jamie turned around to see Archie Fairclough, Hawkstone's assistant manager, standing behind him.

"That's if I'm ever allowed back," said Jamie. There was a tear in his eye, and when he looked at Archie, Jamie could see that he was upset too.

After all, when Jamie had arrived at Hawkstone like an injured puppy, barely able to walk, let alone run, it was Archie who had patiently but brilliantly coaxed him back.

When it looked like Jamie's body had been broken, like he had no future in football, Archie was the one who had fixed him.

Jamie would never forget that. Ever.

But now all their hard work, everything they had achieved together, was going down the drain.

As rain pelted against the roof of the Hawkstone training ground, the pair of them stood in silence for a second or two.

"I don't understand why he's doing this," Jamie said, his voice breaking. "Why is he sending me away, Archie?"

Archie Fairclough pursed his lips. It looked as though he wanted to say something but didn't know how.

"Sometimes, Jamie," he said, trying to find the words he needed. "Sometimes . . . things happen for a reason. We don't know why at the time, but when we look back . . . when we see things for what they really were . . . then we understand."

"I don't even know what you're talking about, Archie," said Jamie, putting his bag over his shoulder as he prepared to walk out of the Hawkstone training ground. "All I know is that I love this club. And now I'm being chucked out."

"Look, Jamie," said Archie firmly. "You've been through worse than this and come back from it. So get your head down, work hard and just make sure you get back here as quickly as you can. OK?"

Jamie turned and looked at Archie. He knew how much Archie wanted him to succeed.

"OK," said Jamie. "See you around, Archie."

"Hey!" shouted Archie, as Jamie opened the door to leave. "Remember . . . never bet against Jamie Johnson."

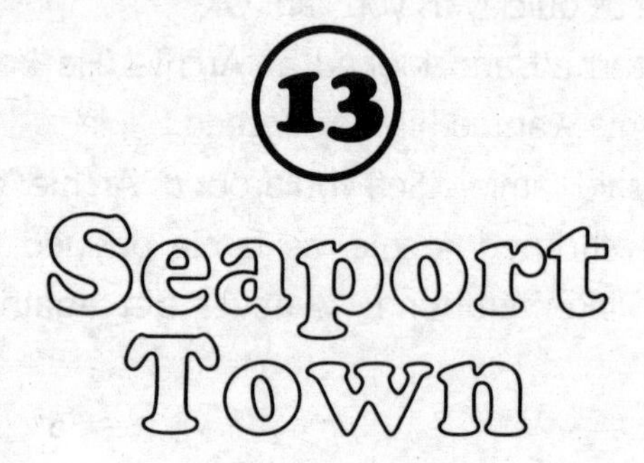

"Raymond Porlock," announced the man, extending his hand to shake Jamie's.

Jamie was having his first meeting with his new manager, Raymond Porlock, boss of Seaport Town. He'd spent the last ten minutes waiting for Porlock, listening to the sound of rats scurrying beneath the floorboards.

Now they were sitting in Porlock's office, and for a moment, there was silence as the player and the manager stared at each other across the desk.

Porlock had a face unlike any that Jamie had ever seen before. He was old – at least fifty, maybe sixty –

and his face was wrinkled and weathered. How many nights must Porlock have stood on the touchlines, in the freezing cold, bellowing out instructions to his players, trying to eke out that extra ten per cent? He had seen everything that football had to offer.

And yet, at the same time, his eyes were fresh, sharp and playful. They were alive with ideas, bright with enthusiasm.

The word in the game was that Raymond Porlock was also slightly eccentric. Had his own way of doing things. Or, to put it another way, he was as mad as a box of frogs.

"Now, what happened at Hawkstone, James . . . I want you to forget all about that," Porlock was saying.

"Jamie," said Jamie.

"What?" asked Porlock.

"My name's Jamie."

"I know what your name is," said Porlock. "But we all have nicknames here. Yours will be James. Now, where was I? Yes, this is a new start for you, James. A new dawn. I want Seaport Town to be the place where you get back to your best. And that will be good for everyone. If you can get back to playing how we both know you can, then that will be great for you and cracking for Seaport Town! Back of the net, eh?"

"Yup . . . back of the net," Jamie said, smiling. But

inside, he was thinking: *Just get me back to Hawkstone. As soon as possible!*

"Morning, lads, gather in," said Raymond Porlock, marching into the dressing room the next morning. He looked odd. He was wearing a lime-green tracksuit top and he'd paired it with bright blue tracksuit bottoms, one grey sock, and one pink one.

'Right, it's Albiston Athletic tomorrow," said Porlock in his husky, croaky voice. "It's the big one; could be ten thousand people watching."

Jamie tried to recall the biggest crowd he'd played in front of. Probably fifty thousand.

"So, by way of preparation, what I want you all to do between now and tomorrow's game is . . . and this is important . . . I want you to imagine all the Albiston players – the entire team – on the toilet."

The Seaport players all dissolved into laughter. Even Jamie.

"Seriously, Mr Porlock?" they teased. "So shall we imagine them going for a wee or a number two?!"

Raymond Porlock held up his hand to quell the chuckles.

"Gentlemen . . . gentlemen . . . I'll have you know that I've been studying a bit of psychology in my spare time, and one of the books that I read clearly states that if you are going into a situation that is making you nervous, just imagine your opponents sitting on the toilet. It makes them less intimidating . . . more, you know, human.

"Listen, lads," he said, aware that the giggles were starting up again. "Trust me, it's all this modern claptrap that'll get us promoted . . . I swear!"

Jamie felt like standing up and saying, "I'm sorry, I don't think I should be at this club. I need to get back to Hawkstone now," and walking straight out of the door.

But Jamie stayed sitting down. As a leak from the ceiling continued to drop cold, dirty water on to his forehead, he bit his lip so hard that he could start to feel the hot, sickly taste of his own blood in his mouth.

It was his big mouth that had got him into this situation in the first place. And he'd decided to keep it firmly shut from now on. He hadn't even told Jack the real story about Bertorelli even though normally they told each other everything.

No. Harry Armstrong had made it very clear – Jamie had to keep his mouth shut and his head down if he ever wanted to play for Hawkstone again.

He had fallen a long way. But the journey back was even further.

"Some of you may have noticed that we have a new face in the dressing room today," Porlock said as the Seaport squad got ready to head outside for training. "We've taken James Johnson on loan from Hawkstone United and he goes straight into the side for tomorrow's match."

Jamie could feel his cheeks start to burn as he sensed the other players turning around to stare at him. Some would be pleased that he was here. Some would not.

"James will be playing right wing," Porlock concluded, almost as an afterthought.

Jamie looked up immediately. He was startled. The whole point of him being at Seaport was to prove to everyone that he was still the best young left-winger in the country.

But how could he do that by playing on the right?

14 Wrong Wing

Dog poo. And lots of it. That was what struck Jamie first about Seaport Town's training pitches.

They were everywhere! Old ones, which were greying, crumbling, decomposing almost to nothing. And new ones. Moist, steaming, brown, smelly new ones.

Jamie had already decided that he wouldn't be making any sliding tackles today!

As the Seaport players made their way out into the pouring rain for training, Jamie caught up with Raymond Porlock. He knew he had to sort out his position in the team as quickly as possible. He just hoped Porlock would see sense.

"Er, gaffer," Jamie said. "Just wanted to let you

know you might have made a bit of a mistake back there earlier."

"Did I indeed, James?" smiled Porlock. "Wouldn't be the first time!"

"Yeah," laughed Jamie. "Erm, it's just you said I would be playing right wing. . ."

"Did I?" said Porlock, now laughing too. In fact, they were both laughing hard.

And then, abruptly, Porlock stopped laughing. His face suddenly looked deadly serious.

"And what was the mistake I made?"

"Well, you know I'm a left-winger?" said Jamie. "I don't play right wing."

"James, you are a footballer, are you not?" asked Porlock, continuing before Jamie could answer. "Of course you can play right wing. I've thought about it. Got it all worked out. If you play right wing, not only will you score more goals because you can cut in and shoot with your left foot, but it will also improve your overall game because it will make you more comfortable on your right. It'll make you twice the player!"

Porlock's excitement was in complete contrast to Jamie's utter deflation. He was starting to get seriously worried.

"Listen . . . gaffer . . . I've played left wing all my life. Never played anywhere else apart from left-wing back once, and that was a bad idea anyway. I mean, don't forget, I've just been playing left wing for Hawkstone in the Premier League.'

Jamie smiled. He didn't think Porlock could argue with that!

"Go on, just play me in my best position. Please, Ray! It'll be—"

"Have you finished?" asked Raymond Porlock. And when Jamie looked up, he could see that something had changed in his manager's eyes. Gone altogether was the jokey spark. Now his eyes were hard. Hard as stone.

"Yes," said Jamie as an icy dagger of wind from the sea suddenly stabbed him right through his shirt.

"Good. Then maybe we'd better get a couple of things straight between us. You may only be at this club on loan. But as long as you *are* here, you will be treated and behave like every other player at this football club.

"That means, a), you will play *exactly* where I tell you to play and b), you only – and I mean ONLY EVER – refer to me as *Mr* Porlock. *Capische?*"

"What?" asked Jamie timidly. He was in shock at how Porlock had changed from mad funny to mad scary in the space of seconds.

"DO YOU UNDERSTAND ME?" Porlock shouted. It was so loud that a flock of birds in a tree above their heads all flew away.

"Yes . . . Mr Porlock," murmured Jamie.

"Good. Then perhaps you and I are beginning to understand each other. So, let me ask you again: what position are you going to play tomorrow?"

This is a test, Jamie thought to himself. *Mustn't crack. Got to stay focused. Have to work my way back up. One more mistake and I'm in trouble. Big trouble.*

"I'll play on the right wing, Mr Porlock," Jamie somehow managed to spit out. "I'll play anywhere you want me to play."

"Well done, James," said Porlock. "That is the correct answer."

15 Jamie's Seaport Debut

Saturday 23 January

"Where's the long-sleeved shirts, mate?" Jamie asked the Seaport Town kit man.

As he pulled on his long-sleeved blue-and-white-striped top, Jamie was aware of the muffled sounds of laughter from the other Seaport players, who were all in short sleeves, despite the cold.

"What?" Jamie laughed. "It's like minus ten out there! Just cos you lot don't mind freezing doesn't mean I have to as well!"

Seaport Town v Albiston Athletic

Even before Jamie got the ball, he'd already decided

what he was going to do. He was a Premier League player. It was showtime.

Jamie flicked the ball into the air and started running with it. He was doing keep-ups as he went. Keep-ups with his knee, his thigh, his he—

BANG!

Jamie had been decked. It wasn't so much a tackle as an assault! And play had been allowed to go on. It wasn't even a free-kick!

"Ref!" Jamie roared, leaping up and chasing after the official. "Ref, what's going on? That would be a sending-off in the Premier League! The geezer almost sliced my chest open!"

The referee didn't even look at Jamie as he simply responded: "We're not playing in the Premier League now."

Seaport Town 0 - 1 Albiston Athletic
Jevons, 54

60 MINS PLAYED

Even in his long-sleeved shirt, Jamie was freezing. He couldn't imagine what the others felt like. His teeth were actually starting to chatter. He had to keep moving just to stop his body freezing up.

"Yes!" he shouted, running into acres of space down the line. "Play me in!"

Receiving the ball, Jamie drove forward a few yards and then quickly back-heeled it behind him. He assumed the full-back would be supporting him. He'd seen the Brazil players do it loads of times.

But the Seaport Town full-back was not there. He was twenty yards behind.

Jamie flung his arms up into the air in frustration.

He looked to the dugout for help. He couldn't do this by himself. He needed someone to work with. A player who could read his game. Who was on his level.

Quickly there was some activity on the Seaport bench. They were making a substitution. *Finally!* Jamie thought. And then he saw the number they were holding up.

At first Jamie couldn't believe it. Thought they had made a mistake holding up his number, but the serious look on Porlock's face told him this was no mistake. He wanted Jamie off.

"You're taking me off?" Jamie shouted across the pitch, his voice thundering with aggression and disappointment. "Why me?"

Jamie was fuming. As he stormed past the dugout, he ripped off his Seaport Town shirt and chucked it angrily right at the feet of Raymond Porlock.

"You know what you can do with that!" he shouted, spitting his words at Porlock.

Almost as soon as he had done it, Jamie regretted it. Sometimes he couldn't help it. The red mist descended and he said things without even knowing what was coming out of his mouth. He knew what he'd done was wrong but he'd been too angry to stop himself.

Jamie kicked the door to the dressing room open and sat down.

He shook his head.

How had it come to this? Where had it all gone wrong? And what kind of footballer was he becoming?

16 Rotten Apple

Monday 25 January

"One more chance, James," said Raymond Porlock, who had gathered the whole Seaport squad together for a team meeting.

"I mean it," he continued, singling Jamie out in front of all the other players as if he were a naughty schoolboy.

"One more strike and you're out. I can't put it any more simply than that. A football team is like a family. We're all in it together. The players, the coaches, the fans. All of us, pulling in the same direction.

"So we can't allow one rotten apple into our barrel. Because if we do, soon enough, we'll all be rotten to the core. We'll all be mouldy, squelchy apples – and that is not what we want to become.

"Are you a rotten apple, James? Is that what you are?"

"No, Mr Porlock," said Jamie, looking at the floor. "I'm not. And I'm sorry. It won't happen again."

"Good," said Porlock. "Then we can try to put the weekend's little outburst behind us. Anyway, as it happens, the reason that I've called this meeting has absolutely nothing to do with that. As you all know, we've been struggling with getting the ball in the back of the old net recently, so I've done something about it . . . I've gone and bought myself a new striker."

All the Seaport players looked at each other. They were not expecting this.

"I've gone back to my old mate, Harry Armstrong at Hawkstone," Porlock continued, "and I've done a deal with him for one of their reserve team players that Harry was prepared to let go.

"They were playing him at the back and I can see why – big lad, great in the air – but I reckon they've missed a trick with him. I reckon if you stick him up the other end, especially in this league, he can be the perfect centre forward. . ."

It was at that moment that Jamie's stomach lurched. He suddenly felt horribly, violently sick. His skin tightened and the acid rose within him. Somehow, he knew what was coming next. . .

"The lad's name is Dillon Simmonds."

Dillon Simmonds was the biggest enemy in Jamie's life.

He had been since Jamie's first day at Kingfield School, when Dillon, the school bully, had singled Jamie out for "treatment".

He'd mocked Jamie for being really small and then, over the next few weeks, months and years, he'd done everything he could to make Jamie's life a misery.

He'd beaten Jamie up a few times and regularly stolen money from him, but worst of all was the way he'd teased Jamie. Continually. Mercilessly.

"Just cos you're too poor to get proper football boots!" he would say. And: "You're such a saddo – no wonder your dad left you!"

It had made Jamie feel like a piece of dirt. In the end, after Dillon had insulted Jamie so many times, even Jamie started to believe what Dillon was saying. He began to hate himself and his family for giving Dillon an excuse to torment him.

To this day, Jamie still didn't know why Dillon had done it. He knew Dillon had problems at home. But that was no excuse. It didn't give him the right to go around bullying people like he did.

They had hardly spoken a word to each other in the time they'd both been at Hawkstone because Jamie was in the first team and Dillon had been in the reserves.

But now Dillon Simmonds was about to come back into Jamie's life.

Just when he least needed him. . .

"Well, whaddaya know?" laughed Dillon, slapping Jamie painfully hard on the back before training the next day. He'd swaggered into Seaport Town like he owned the place. "Jamie Johnson, you follow me everywhere!"

Jamie turned around to see that Dillon was holding out his hand to shake Jamie's.

Not that Jamie was going to fall for that old trick again. The amount of times Dillon had pretended to shake Jamie's hand in the playground and then either drawn it away at the last moment – to leave Jamie looking like a fool – or, worse still, had taken Jamie's hand and crushed the knuckles together so hard that you could actually hear them crack.

Jamie would never fall for that trick again. He would never shake Dillon Simmonds' hand as long as they were both alive.

"I was here first," Jamie shot back, deliberately ignoring Dillon's hand. "So how can *I* be the one following *you*?"

Saturday 30 January

Mortsmouth City v Seaport Town

"Just give it to me," Dillon said as he and Jamie stood over the ball before kick-off. "Everyone knows you've lost it."

Jamie ground his teeth. It was true. Everyone thought he'd lost it.

But Jamie knew it was all still there. Everything. The skill, the pace, the tricks. . .

He still had it all.

And now was the time to prove it.

Jamie took the centre by knocking the ball into Dillon's feet. Then, as soon as Dillon had touched the ball, Jamie nicked it back and immediately set off on a run.

There were eleven players between him and the goal of his life.

But Jamie didn't care. He knew he could do this. He could go all the way himself. . .

A step-over and he was past one defender, a burst of raw pace and he was through the middle of two other challenges as if they didn't exist. Now a body-swerve and he was through to the edge of the area.

The opposition was dissolving in front of Jamie, paving the way for him to score a wonder goal. Porlock was off his seat; the entire crowd stood in suspense, waiting to witness a potential moment of football history. . .

Now a double drag-back to beat the last defender. A blur of electric skill and Jamie was past him, racing forward . . . until he suddenly found himself being jerked backwards as if by some magnetic current.

Instead of powering on and lashing the ball home, he tumbled to the ground, screaming in frustration.

The defender had grabbed Jamie's shirt and yanked him down just outside the edge of the area.

Jamie leapt up, like a boxer looking for a fight. Had he been allowed to finish off the goal, it would have been one of the best he'd ever scored. That chance had been stolen from him.

But there was no way he was going to let anyone else take this free-kick. If he curled it right into the top corner it might still turn out to be his ticket back to the Premier L—

"I'll take the free-kick!" announced Dillon Simmonds, grabbing the ball and shoving Jamie forcefully out of the way. "I need the goals."

Jamie felt the anger lift from his chest into his arms. He felt the rage overtake him and, before he could stop himself, he was aiming a furious shove straight back in the direction of Dillon Simmonds.

"Why do you need the goals more than me?!" Jamie roared as he lashed out. "It's *my* free-kick!"

He pushed at Dillon's body with all his might and he was surprised at how light Dillon's frame seemed. Too light. . .

Immediately Jamie sensed that something was wrong. He'd got into enough tussles with Dillon over the years to know that this was not Dillon's chest he was shoving.

It was not Dillon Simmonds at all. It was the referee, who, without Jamie realizing, had placed himself between him and Dillon when tempers had started to flare. But with fury blinding him, Jamie had launched himself at the nearest person to him, assuming it was Dillon.

With every bit of strength he had in his body, Jamie had just pushed the referee right in the chest.

And now, almost in slow motion, the referee was desperately trying to stay on his feet. His arms were wheeling up into the air as he staggered backwards. But it was a losing battle; he looked as though he were roller skating on ice!

It looked funny. Hilarious, even. As the ref's legs finally buckled and he fell over, some of the players were even laughing.

But when the ref hit the back of his head on the hard frozen ground, they stopped laughing. There was such a loud thud that the players knew it must have hurt. Badly.

For a second, nothing happened. No one had ever seen anything like this happen before.

Then, coming to his senses, Jamie rushed over to the ref to apologize.

"Ref!" he shouted. "Sorry, mate. I didn't know it was you, honest! Ref?"

But the man in black was out cold. The physios from both teams had to prop him up and wipe his face with a wet sponge before he began to come back round.

Jamie was in shock. He watched as the referee was hauled off the pitch on a stretcher. The poor man had no idea where he was. He looked as though someone had just woken him up from a coma.

After a brief discussion on the touchline, the fourth official marched on to the pitch to take over the referee's duties.

And his very first action was to stride over to Jamie and instantly show him the red card.

Jamie wanted to argue. He wanted to say that it wasn't his fault; Dillon was the one who had started it. That he would never have pushed the referee on purpose. That this was all another one of Dillon's plans to get him.

But he knew there was no point. They were never going to change their minds. He kept his mouth shut and trudged slowly, silently off the pitch.

Jamie Johnson had been sent off after exactly two minutes and thirty-one seconds.

footballtalk.com

HOME | ALL THE NEWS | TEAMS | FIXTURES & RESULTS | STATISTICS

Shameful Assault on Referee Rocks Football World

The career of football's former golden boy, Jamie Johnson, was hanging by a thread last night after the winger knocked out a referee.

Johnson, on loan at Division 1 outfit Seaport Town from Premier League side Hawkstone United, lost his temper in yesterday's match.

After only two minutes, Johnson launched a senseless attack on referee Arthur Salcock, knocking the highly respected official unconscious.

Johnson is set to be banned and fined by the football authorities, while his manager at Seaport, Raymond Porlock, also had strong words for the disgraced winger.

"This is not acceptable. Full stop," Porlock admitted. "Referees are the lifeblood of football. We need them more than they need us. It'll be a long time before he pulls on a Seaport Town shirt again."

Jamie stared at the screen on his mobile in disbelief.

He hadn't wanted any of this. None of it. All he'd ever wanted was to play football.

But now he'd been banned. When would he be allowed to kick a ball again?

19 Ball Games

Friday 26 February

Although it only been four weeks, Jamie felt as though he hadn't played football for years. Decades, even.

Despite the fact that his ban would soon be over, Raymond Porlock had said that he still had no intention of picking Jamie for Seaport Town. He didn't think Jamie was "mentally ready" to come back yet.

Above everything else, Jamie missed the buzz. Nothing on earth felt as good as playing football.

To stay fit, Jamie had been going for long runs by himself every day.

He sprinted up and down the streets around his house, each day setting himself new targets to keep pushing himself to the limit.

Sometimes, like today, he even went down to the main road so that he could run on the pavement and race against the cars.

Jamie was sprinting as fast as he could, trying to keep pace with an old Mercedes, when he suddenly stopped. Something had caught his eye.

He'd seen a massive poster on the street. It was of Mattheus Bertorelli, posing, advertising a very expensive brand of sunglasses.

Just seeing Bertorelli's smarmy, smug, cheating face had sent a spear of pain and anger through Jamie. Burning with frustration, he started to tear down the poster there and then. He wanted to get rid of it.

Soon, as he ripped away at the paper, the poster hidden underneath began to become visible.

When he saw it, Jamie froze. Shocked.

The poster buried underneath was the one for Nemesis football boots. As worn by Jamie Johnson.

Jamie stared at his own image.

The image of Jamie Johnson – yesterday's hero.

Jamie felt like going home and had just taken a shortcut through the estate when – *WHACK!* – he was smashed in the face by something hard and wet.

He looked down to see possibly the ugliest old tennis ball that he had ever come across. The ball was completely bald, shorn of all the green fur that had once covered it. Now it simply looked like a bouncy brown plastic potato!

Jamie picked it up and was just about to send it skyward with a huge volley when a voice called out to him.

"Oi! Mate! That's my ball! Chuck it back here, will ya!"

Jamie looked around to see a kid, probably no more than ten years old, scampering towards him.

Jamie smiled as the boy got nearer.

"You looking for this?" said Jamie, holding the ball just too high for the boy to reach.

"Oi! Give it back!" barked the boy, desperately trying to jump high enough to snatch it back out of Jamie's hand.

The boy was really tiny. Only came up to Jamie's hip. His tracksuit bottoms were frayed at the knee and at the heel, and even though it was freezing, he was just wearing a small T-shirt, which looked as if it had never been washed. The kid also had a shaved head and gleaming little stud earrings in both his ears.

"OK!" announced the kid, finally giving up on trying to get the ball out of Jamie's hands. "I'll play you for the ball, then! I'll smash you!"

"You want to play me?" smiled Jamie. He liked this kid. He reminded him of someone. "And you think you'll smash me?"

"You best believe it," said the kid. "I'm gonna teach you a lesson!"

20 Robbed!

It was the first to five and Jamie let the kid have the first four goals.

He's a good kid, Jamie thought to himself. *A bit cocky, maybe . . . but he definitely reminds me of someone. Anyway, now it's time to show him who's boss. . .*

And with that, Jamie instantly turned on the skill, pulling three goals back straight away.

Then, at 3-4 down, Jamie produced a wicked double drag-back to equalize with a goal that even shut the kid up for a couple of seconds.

"Whoa!" said the kid, in awe. "Double drag-back! That's the best skill ever! You've got to teach me how to do that!"

"Maybe some other time," said Jamie. "We're in the middle of a game here. Four-four. Next goal wins!"

Jamie wiped the sweat from his forehead. Never mind that he was playing against a kid in the street with an old tennis ball; it felt great just to be playing football again. It had been over a month since he'd played. He'd pulled it back and was going to win, but it hadn't been easy. He'd had to put some effort into it.

Now the kid was dribbling slowly out of his goal, but as Jamie advanced to tackle him, the kid's eyes suddenly widened. His face transformed into a picture of surprise.

"What the. . ." said the kid, pointing behind Jamie.

Jamie turned around quickly to see what it was. But he couldn't see anything. There was nothing there.

"What were you—" Jamie started to ask, but it was too late. The kid was already gone. He'd sprinted forward while Jamie was looking the other way and now he was an inch away from the cardboard box. Jamie had been done by the oldest trick in the book!

"Yes!" shouted the kid, slotting the ball home. "I win! I told you I would beat you!"

"Well done," smiled Jamie. Inside he was fuming, but he put on a brave face and offered his hand. "What's your name?"

But just as their hands were about to meet, the kid

snatched his hand away and put his thumb on his forehead, wiggling his fingers!

"Beat you again," he shouted. "My name's Robbie."

"I'll have to keep an eye on you, Robbie. I'm Jamie."

It was then that they both heard a familiar voice echo their way from the end of the street.

"RRRROOOOBBBBIIIIEEE!" shouted Dillon Simmonds angrily. "Where have you been? I've cooked your dinner – get back home now!"

Jamie and Dillon stared at each other down the street. They hadn't spoken since Jamie had been sent off for pushing the ref when he'd meant to shove Dillon.

"All right! Keep your hair on, fatso!" Robbie shouted and started to sprint towards Dillon.

"Show me the drag-back another time, loser," he shouted over his shoulder to Jamie. "Gotta go before psycho face gets angry!"

"Hey, Robbie!" Jamie called after the little street footballer. "Haven't you forgotten something?"

And with that he hurled the old tennis ball as fast as he could at Robbie Simmonds. He wanted to see how Robbie reacted.

The ball was going about forty miles an hour, but Robbie didn't get out of the way. Instead, he moved towards the ball, chested it up into the air and controlled it on his forehead, before letting it drop down into his open hand.

Well, what do you know? Jamie thought to himself. *Not only does Dillon Simmonds have a younger brother, but the kid's got talent. Serious talent.*

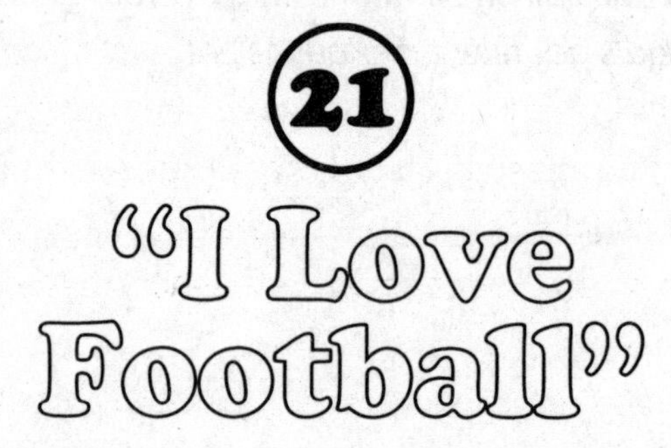

That night Jamie fell into a deep, deep sleep. He was revisiting the same moment that he often dreamt about.

It was the time when he'd been a mascot for Hawkstone United when he was eleven years old. That had been the best day of his life. Jamie had done the most amazing overhead kick in front of a full Hawkstone United crowd!

It had been that day – that moment – that had given Jamie the confidence to believe, perhaps for the first time, that he really could make it as a professional footballer. . .

Except tonight the dream was different. In it, instead of being himself, this time Jamie was a member of the crowd, watching on from the stands.

He was out of his seat, trying to catch a glimpse of what was happening on the pitch. He saw the young mascot flick the ball up and then leap into the air to execute the most perfectly beautiful overhead kick that you could hope to see. The ball flew into the back of the net, as though it was somehow desperate to get there.

The supporters in the stands instinctively rose to their feet and clapped, all of them asking the exact same questions: "Who is that boy? What's his name? He's going to be some player. . ."

And then Jamie saw the boy turn to each corner of the ground and drink in their applause.

But in tonight's dream, when the boy turned around, when he finally revealed his face, it was not Jamie's eleven-year-old features that he saw. Instead it was those of the little kid he had met today, Robbie.

In the dream, it was now Robbie who was lost in the joy of scoring a goal, bouncing around in ecstasy shouting the words, "I love football! I love football!" exactly as Jamie had done that day.

Jamie woke up with a jolt. It was a jolt of both fear and realization.

Fear that he might be letting his football career slip through his fingers.

And realization of exactly what had been missing from his game for the last few months. What it was that he had lost.

It was his love for football.

22 "Let Me Play"

Monday 1 March

"I'm not interested, James," said Raymond Porlock before Jamie had even begun his speech.

"I know your ban's finished. But that doesn't make any difference to me. I do what's best for this football club. And at the moment, that does not include picking you. End of story."

Jamie nodded. "I know," he said. "And you're right, Mr Porlock. Like you said: the team comes first. There's just a few things I think I need to say. Need to get them off my chest. It'll only take a couple of minutes . . . will you just hear me out?"

Porlock took off his glasses and rested them on his

desk. "Go on, then," he said and, with a wave of his hand, motioned for Jamie to continue.

For a second Jamie shuffled nervously from one foot to the other. He felt as though he were in a school play and he'd forgotten his lines. When he'd walked into Porlock's office he'd known exactly what he'd wanted to say, but now his mind had gone blank. He couldn't access a single word.

"Well, come on, then!" ordered Porlock. "Stop prancing around like you're in Riverdance and get on with it!"

"Well. . . What it is, Mr Porlock," started Jamie. "The last few days I've been, like, asking myself what I would be doing if I wasn't a footballer. Maybe I'd be working in a sports shop, maybe I'd be a PE teacher, I don't know, maybe I'd be a bin man. . . But my point is, whatever else I could do, nothing would be as good as being a footballer . . . and that's not cos of the money, or being famous. It's because I love it."

Jamie tried to remember the last time he had actually scored in a match. It had been too long. Way too long.

"Playing football – it's the only thing I can do, Mr Porlock. The only thing I want to do. So let me play for Seaport Town again. Please . . . I'll play anywhere you want me – in goal, I don't care – just let me play football again. Let me show you what I can really do."

Raymond Porlock rested his elbows on his desk, linked his hands together and put his chin on his knuckles.

Then he let out a deep, long sigh.

"Would the real James Johnson please stand up?" he said.

"What?" Jamie frowned. "I don't under—"

"I think, if I'm not mistaken, that a real professional footballer has just walked into my office," said Raymond Porlock with a huge smile.

"Welcome back, James. Welcome back."

23 First Game Back

Saturday 6 March

Northend United v Seaport Town

As the game kicked off, Jamie's heart began to pound with excitement. He could feel his spirit awaken and his legs and feet come alive in a way that they had not done in months.

He was ready to play.

And the first time he received the ball, he knew exactly what to do. He pushed the ball in front of him and rocketed forward, soaring down the line. He could feel the wind battering his ears. He seemed to be running so fast he might take off.

Two, then three players came across and tried to stop him in any way they could. A flying lunge, a pull of the shirt, a rugby tackle, even. But nothing was going to stop Jamie Johnson today. Nothing in the world.

Jamie got to the byline on the right-hand touchline and without thinking, he wrapped his right foot around the ball to curl a glorious centre into the box. It was as sweet a cross as any he had ever made with his left foot.

With pace and whip and curl, the ball arrowed to the far post, where Dillon Simmonds launched himself powerfully, bravely into the air and nodded the ball down and into the net.

It was an awesome goal.

Seaport Town were ahead after four minutes and twenty-nine seconds.

Northend United 0 - 1 Seaport Town
D Simmonds, 5

Jamie looked to the dugout to see Raymond Porlock, dressed as ever in his bright green jumper, wheeling down the line with his arms outstretched. He was running towards the Seaport Town fans, leaning from side to side as he went. He was doing the aeroplane celebration!

The Seaport players split into two groups, half of them gathering around Dillon to congratulate him on his strike, half of them patting Jamie on the back. They were fully aware that not many players in football could run down the line and put in a cross like that.

But the celebrations didn't last for too long. Quickly the Seaport players jogged back to the centre circle. There was a hunger in the air. An appetite for more goals.

As they jogged past each other and prepared for the restart, Jamie Johnson and Dillon Simmonds made eye contact with each other.

"Good ball," snarled Dillon without a hint of joy. It looked as though it physically hurt him to say the words.

"Nice finish," spat Jamie.

He wanted to wash his mouth out as soon as he'd said it.

Right from the kick-off, the Seaport Town players charged forward. They were a unit, working as one. They ran, chased and harried, forcing an error from their opponents.

Finally, a midfielder attempted to pass the ball back to his central defender, but his contact with the ball was too weak.

The ball was there for the taking.

Jamie raced in from the wing and took possession. Then he stopped and pretended he was about to back-heel the ball behind him. But as soon as he saw the defender falling for his trick, Jamie knocked the ball forward instead and scampered after it.

He swiftly outpaced two markers and then, on the edge of the area, he nutmegged the final defender!

He was so happy to be back playing he could actually feel himself smiling as he powered forward now, one on one with the keeper.

He knew he could beat this keeper in any way he wanted: a volley, a curler, a side-foot into the corner . . . he even had time to set himself up for an overhead.

But he just wanted to get the ball into the back of the net as quickly as possible.

He looked down at the ball and, with his left foot, simply lashed it home. He wellied it, stonked it, absolutely hammered it! And the ball thundered right into the top corner!

Jamie couldn't contain his adrenaline.

"Boom!" he roared. "Pick that one out!"

Jamie was making up for lost time.

It may have been 2-0 to Seaport, but Jamie Johnson was only just getting started. . .

Northend United 0 - 2 Seaport Town

D Simmonds, 5

J Johnson, 9

Seaport Town went on to win the game 9-2! It was the biggest away league win in their history!

FULL-TIME

Northend United 2 - 9 Seaport Town

G Morgan, 38	D Simmonds, 5, 28, 34, 67
A Renton, 80	J Baptista, 54
	J Johnson, 9, 71
	W Scrimshaw (O.G.), 78
	S Cribbins, 62

At the end of the game, as they walked off the pitch, the Seaport players couldn't help but laugh.

Their left-winger, Stuart Cribbins, the club joker, was doing the robot dance as his teammates got in a circle around him and clapped his moves!

"That's it, Stu!" they shouted, egging him on. "Throw us some shapes!"

Meanwhile, Raymond Porlock had jumped into the crowd and was now singing with the rest of the fans: "*Ten goals! We only wanted ten goals . . . we only wanted ten goals . . . we only wanted ten goals. . . Ten goals. . .*"

"Whenever You're Ready"

"Phenomenal, James!" said Raymond Porlock, as soon as they got into the dressing room after the game. "You were quicker than three leopards driving a Ferrari! No! Make that four!"

"Cheers, Mr Porlock!" said Jamie, laughing. "Feels great to be back."

"Who needs Bertorelli when you've got James Johnson, eh?" gloated Porlock.

But as soon as he heard that cheat's name, Jamie's smile instantly vanished. Just thinking about him made Jamie feel like puking on the spot.

*

"So you want to tell me what's up?" asked Raymond Porlock a little while later, as he sat down next to Jamie on the coach back to Seaport.

The rest of the team were having a laugh and playing cards in the back three rows, but Jamie was sitting by himself, near the front, looking aimlessly out of the window.

"Nothing's up," said Jamie, avoiding eye contact with Porlock. He was tracing a raindrop with his finger as it slid down the outside of the window. "I'm fine."

"Do me a favour, son. You play sensationally. I mean really sensationally. World class. You're as happy as Larry and then I mention Mattheus Bertorelli's name and suddenly you close up, go into your shell and don't say a word to anyone. . . Look, you're doing it again!"

Jamie knew the red fury in his cheeks was giving him away. He couldn't help it. Knowing what Bertorelli was planning – and that the game that he was going to get himself sent off in couldn't be too far away now – made Jamie feel like punching a hole right through the side of the bus.

"I just don't like being compared to Bertor. . ." Jamie stopped and clenched his jaw tight. He couldn't say his name. "I don't like being compared to *him,* OK? I'm nothing like him. Nothing like him at all."

"OK, Jamie," Porlock said. "I've got that. So do you

want to level with me, then? Tell me what it is you've got against the guy?"

A bit of Jamie did want to talk about it, wanted to get it out in the open. But he also knew that if he did, he'd never play for Hawkstone again. And that was something he couldn't risk.

"I just . . . don't want to talk about it right now, Mr Porlock," he said. "OK?"

"*Don't* want to or *can't*?" asked Porlock, searching Jamie's eyes for clues. But Jamie remained silent long enough for his manager to realize that the conversation wasn't going any further.

"Fair enough," said Porlock, tapping Jamie's shoulder as he stood up. "But remember, whenever you're ready to talk . . . I'm here."

25 Drag-Backs

Thursday 18 March

"Robbie?!" Jamie shouted. "What are you doing chucking stones at my window? You're gonna break it!"

"Come for you to teach me the double drag-backs, like you said!"

"Fine," said Jamie. "Wait there. I'll be down in a sec."

As Jamie put on his tracksuit bottoms, he realized that he was quite looking forward to this. It had taken him weeks to perfect the double drag-back himself when he was younger.

He was keen to see how long it took Robbie.

"Cos you're right-footed, I'll show you it with the right foot," said Jamie, demonstrating with Robbie's old tennis ball.

"Right. So you're dribbling towards the defender, yeah? Then. . ."

1 *As you approach the defender . . .*

2 *. . . turn your body away from him, dragging the ball back with your right foot.*

3 *Keep turning, stepping over the ball and switching feet to drag the ball back with your left foot this time.*

4 *Now finish the turn and your second drag-back at the same time. . .*

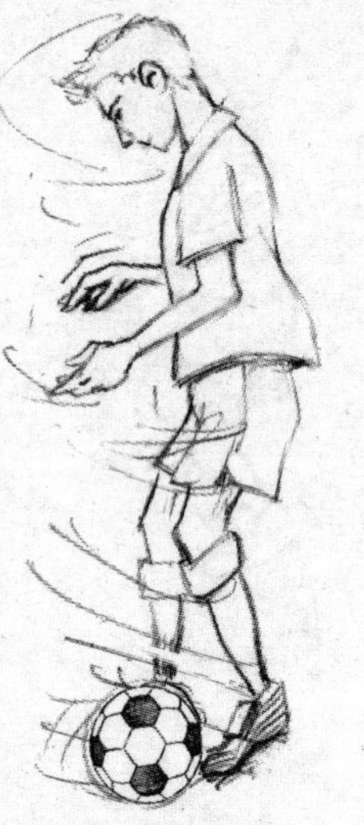

5 *And you'll be facing the way you were originally running.*

6 *But now you've got the defender behind you and the ball in front of you. . .*

7 *So you're ready to accelerate away!*

"That's wicked!" said Robbie "Sick!"

"Exactly!" smiled Jamie. "OK, your turn now. You'll probably muck it up the first time, but don't worry, I did too. It's normal. The main thing is to drag the ball back twice and get the full turn in."

"OK," said Robbie. "You mean like this?"

And with that, Robbie sprinted forward and produced the double drag-back perfectly. First time!

"Yeah," laughed Jamie in amazement. He couldn't work out whether he was more surprised or impressed. "Yeah, exactly like that!"

Jamie and Robbie practised together for about an hour until Robbie suddenly looked at his watch and said: "Gotta go in a minute. Old fatty chops will have my dinner ready."

"What's all this with Dillon and the cooking?" Jamie asked. "Does he want to be one of those TV chefs or something?"

"It's him or no one, innit?" said Robbie. "Just me and fat face now."

"What do you mean just you and him? What about your dad?" Jamie remembered seeing Dillon's dad once. Scary bloke.

"Nah, he died last year," said Robbie without any emotion.

"Oh," said Jamie. "Sorry. I didn't know. What about your mum?"

Robbie looked down at his shoes. They were a grubby pair of old scuffed-up football trainers.

"She's gone to live with some other bloke," he murmured. "Like I said, it's just me and fat face."

As Jamie looked at Robbie, for the first time he saw through all the big talk to the little boy that he still was.

"But you two are all right for money and everything,

yeah?" Jamie asked, looking at the tattered state of Robbie's clothes.

"Kind of. He's not on much at Seaport, but he says that he's got it in his contract that if he scores twenty goals this season, then he gets a bonus. That's why it's good you've started setting up loads of goals!"

Jamie thought about his recent games for Seaport and smiled. Since he'd come back, he'd been playing right wing and he'd done brilliantly.

Porlock had made Jamie and Dillon both stay back together after training to practise. They had both complained bitterly at the prospect of having to spend more time together, but Porlock had insisted.

"I don't care if you don't like each other, couldn't give two hoots," he'd said. "But I want you to know each other's games inside out."

So every day, the two old enemies stayed behind for an hour's extra training. They didn't say a single word to each other. Jamie simply whipped in cross after cross with his ever-improving right foot, while Dillon banged them home from all angles.

It had paid off handsomely too. He and Dillon had scored ten goals between them in the last three games. Seaport had raced up the division and Jamie's form had almost returned to its top level.

"So he's on goal bonuses, is he?" said Jamie,

suddenly thinking back to how keen Dillon had been to take the free-kick that had led to Jamie being sent off for pushing the ref.

It had also given Jamie an idea of how he might be able to do his new mate Robbie a little favour.

"So what's he like then?" asked Stuart Cribbins, Seaport's left-winger. He was one of the best characters in the squad. And certainly the funniest dancer!

The whole of the Seaport Town squad was in the clubhouse watching Hawkstone v Aldwich City, which was live on the TV. It was a big game. Hawkstone had to win it to go second.

Premier League Table

Teams	P	GD	Points
1. Foxborough	26	+35	60
2. Larchester Rangers	27	+28	58
3. Hawkstone United	26	+29	56

It had been Porlock's idea to get all the players and staff together to celebrate Seaport's recent good form. They could even make the play-offs now.

"What's who like, Stu?" asked Jamie, vacantly. He didn't like talking much when Hawkstone were playing. He wanted to watch and remember everything that was going on in the game and he couldn't do that while he was talking.

"Bertorelli," said Cribbins. "What's he like in the dressing room then? Is he as cool as he looks? Has he got women coming out of his ears? Come on, spill the beans!"

Jamie turned to Cribbins. A couple of weeks ago, he might have stood up and punched him. Might have told him never to mention Bertorelli's name again.

But now, right at this moment, Jamie didn't feel angry. In fact, with the way things had been going on the pitch for Seaport and with his form returning so rapidly, Jamie actually felt happier than he had done for a really long time.

"Shall I tell you a secret about Bertorelli?" asked Jamie, pretending to whisper but actually speaking loud enough for the whole of the Seaport squad to hear him.

"Yeah," said Cribbins, his eyes widening like a child about to receive his birthday present. "Yeah, go on, tell us an' all!"

"OK," said Jamie, looking around. "But it's a secret, remember?"

"Yeah, I know," said Cribbins. "Go on, tell us."

"OK," said Jamie. "Well . . . Mattheus Bertorelli is not as cool as he seems. On his bum, right . . . he's got a whole load of spots!"

"What?" laughed Cribbins. There were grins from the growing group of players now surrounding Jamie to catch the gossip.

"Yeah – it's true," said Jamie. "I'm not talking normal spots here, either. I'm talking big, red boils, full of pus! They're so big that they sometimes pop in the shower and squirt everywhere. I'm not joking! Once he said that some had got infected and it was too painful for him to train! He missed training because of boils on his bum! Have you ever heard of that?!"

By now everyone in the room, including Jamie, was bent double, laughing. A couple of the players found it so funny they almost started crying!

Yes, it was all a complete and utter lie, but Jamie didn't care – he was too busy cracking up.

And he realized something else too: he was beginning to feel right at home at Seaport Town.

Jamie was up off his seat before the Hawkstone goal had even gone in.

He knew what was going to happen before anyone else because it was a set-piece they had practised every day in training: Glenn Richardson drifted a corner to the near post, where it was flicked on by Bertorelli. Meanwhile, Rigobert West, a.k.a. The Beast, would make a run to meet the ball at the far post.

The plan had just worked to perfection. It was a winner in the eighty-sixth minute. Hawkstone were going back to second in the Premier League and Jamie Johnson was going a little bit mental. . .

"Oh baby!" he roared, leaping up off his chair as though he'd just been fired from an ejector seat.

Then Jamie tore off his top and revealed that he was wearing his own Hawkstone United shirt underneath. He pulled it over his forehead and started sprinting around the room like an absolute madman. He couldn't see a thing because the shirt was over his eyes. He could have easily run head first into a brick wall!

While the rest of the Seaport players just sat, watched, and mostly laughed at Jamie's rather unusual performance, Jamie concluded his blind sprint with a full-length dive across the carpet of the Seaport Town clubhouse.

"You don't stop The Beast!" he yelled. "I'm tellin' you, you DO NOT stop The Beast!! We are Hawkstone! Say we are Hawkstone!"

27 "Do Something"

"It was a good night," said Raymond Porlock as he and Jamie finished clearing up the clubhouse. "The closer we are off the pitch, the better we are on it."

Jamie had stayed behind to help with the cleaning since he'd been the one who had created most of the mess during his celebrations for the Hawkstone goal. He'd knocked a whole bowl of crisps off the table and now they'd been trampled into the carpet.

Besides, he was sort of getting to enjoy spending time with Raymond Porlock now. He'd realized that often there was actually a whole load of sense behind some of the mad comments his manager made.

"And it's good to see you happy," said Porlock, tying up one of the black bin liners, which was full to the top of empty plastic bottles. "You deserve it."

"Thanks, Mr Porlock," Jamie replied. "Well, I guess if Hawkstone win, I'm happy. Simple as. Always been the same."

Jamie realized now that this would never change. No matter where he was in his life, who he was playing for or how old he got, he would always remain the same thing that he had been since the day Mike had introduced him to football – a Hawkstone United fan.

"You're a good man, James," Porlock smiled. "And you will play for Hawkstone again. I have no doubts about that."

"I hope so," said Jamie. He liked being referred to as a man. "I really hope so."

"And when you do go back there," Porlock enquired, in slightly softer tones, "what about you and Bertorelli? Would you be prepared to play alongside him?"

Jamie sat down. He'd never actually thought that far ahead.

"I don't know," he replied. "I don't think I can answer that question."

"That bad, eh?" said Porlock, drawing a chair up alongside Jamie's. "What he did was really that bad?"

Jamie nodded. Then he sighed.

"Even if I did tell you, you probably wouldn't believe me."

"Try me," said Raymond Porlock.

Jamie told Raymond Porlock everything. How he'd heard Bertorelli arranging to fix a match. How they'd got into a fight at the training ground. And how Harry Armstrong had told him that, if he ever breathed a word of it to anyone, he'd never play for Hawkstone again.

And now the two of them were sitting next to each other, with only the truth in between them.

"That's a lot to carry around on your shoulders, James," said Porlock, sympathy in his voice.

"So you believe me?" said Jamie.

"Of course I believe you. The question is, what are you going to do about it?"

"Nothing," said Jamie. "What can *I* do? Harry Armstrong says I'll never play for Hawkstone again."

Raymond Porlock shook his head.

"Seems to me, James, that you don't really have too much of a choice. You have to do something."

"Me? Why?"

"Think about it. This little problem can go one of two ways: either the guy and whoever he's working with pull it off – in which case Hawkstone lose a massive game, probably the league title too, and he leaves the club and gets away with it . . . or . . . he gets found out after it's too late.

"Then the whole of football comes under suspicion – I'm talking about every single game that gets played, people are going to wonder whether it's been fixed – and Hawkstone United will for ever be known as the club that threw a game. Either of those outcomes sound any good to you?"

"But what about what Harry said?" asked Jamie. "Who knows? Maybe he's even in on it too."

Porlock flicked his hand out as if swatting an imaginary fly.

"Harry Armstrong did what any manager would have done. He tried to protect his dressing room. Tried to protect the team unit. Look at it from his point of view: far easier to send you out on loan and keep the team together than believe his star player – and new signing, don't forget that – is planning to fix a game."

Raymond Porlock took in a deep breath of air. His eyes were darting everywhere, searching for ideas. Searching for answers.

"But believe me," he said. "I go back a long way with Harry. He's as honest as the day is long and he loves football as much as anyone. If he knew the truth, he'd want you to do something. Not for your sake. Not even for Hawkstone's sake. But for football's sake."

"But what?" asked Jamie. "What do I do? Who do I go to? The police?"

Porlock shook his head.

"No time for that. It'll take too long. You need to speak to someone who can act quickly. Before it's too late."

"Like who?" said Jamie. "That's what I'm saying – if I knew someone like that, then I would have gone to them in the first place, wouldn't I?"

"Think, James," insisted Porlock. "There must be someone. I can't do it. I'm in football. Too close to it all. It needs to be someone on the outside. And above all, it needs to be someone who you can trust."

Jamie thought for a second.

"Well," he said, finally . . . hesitantly. "There is *one* person. . ."

Someone to Trust

Jamie made the call. Then he hung up. Then he made the call again. This time he let it ring. . .

He knew this was a risk. A massive risk. But he couldn't think of any other way.

"Hi, JJ," said the voice at the other end.

"Hi, Jack," said Jamie. "I'm calling because I need your help. . ."

There was a long, painful silence.

Jamie had just told Jack everything. Jack had hardly said a word during the entire phone call. She'd just let Jamie talk. And as he'd told his story, Jamie had become increasingly aware of how far-fetched it all sounded. Match-fixing, throwing a game to make millions. . . Jamie knew that if the roles had been reversed, if this had been Jack telling him the exact same story, he'd have struggled to believe her.

He even started to doubt himself. Had he really remembered it all exactly as it had happened? Or had he imagined some of it? Part of it? All of it? Was he really a hundred per cent sure that Mattheus Bertorelli, one of the biggest stars in football, was a cheat?

"You're an idiot, Jamie," said Jack, sharply.

"See, I knew it!" shouted Jamie. "I knew you wouldn't believe me! You think I'm just making this up cos I'm jealous of him, don't you? Well I'm not! He's a cheat! He's a fake, and by the time you see, it'll be too late. He'll have ruined everyth—"

"Jamie! Calm down!" Jack responded, a cool confidence in her voice. "You're an idiot for not telling me sooner. . . Of course I believe you."

"Oh," said Jamie. "Right. . . OK, then. So, what are we going to do?"

Another silence. Jamie could almost hear Jack's mind working. Quickly. Intelligently.

"Leave it with me," she said. "I need to do some digging. Find out more. I'll get back to you."

"OK. But be quick. The match could be anytime."

"I will, don't worry. See you later, Jamie."

"Jack, wait . . . do you reckon you can stop this thing happening?"

"You know me, Jamie, once I put my mind to something—"

"Yeah, I know," smiled Jamie. "You don't let go until you win. But be careful, Jack. These guys could be dangerous."

"I can look after myself," said Jack. "And anyway, that's the exciting part! Listen, don't worry, I'm on it. Probably best that we don't speak about it for a while, though. We should keep you out of this."

"Cool," said Jamie. "Thanks, Jack."

"No probs – I'll get to the bottom of it. . . And Jamie?"

"Yeah?"

"You did the right thing calling me."

Jamie smiled as he put down the phone.

If there was one person in this world who he trusted, it was Jacqueline Alexandra Marshall.

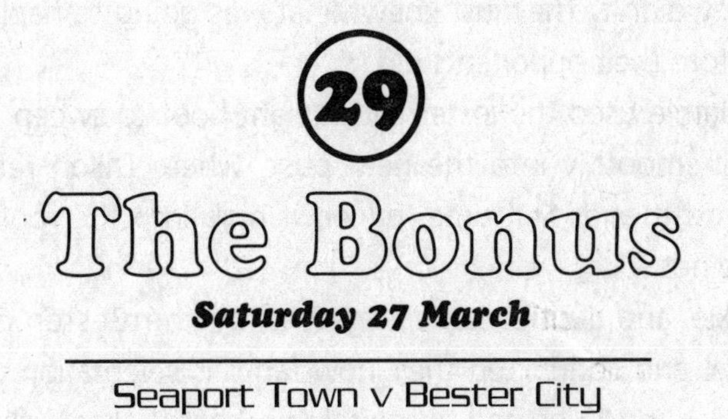

29
The Bonus

Saturday 27 March

Seaport Town v Bester City

Jamie skipped down the line. He galloped past the last defender like a racehorse jumping the final hurdle in a big race. Now he was level with the edge of the box. . .

He didn't even have to look up. Both he and Dillon knew the plan that Porlock had given them. If Jamie crossed as soon as he got level with the penalty area, his centre would be along the ground to the near post – Dillon's job was to get across the front defender and sweep in a shot. But if Jamie went all the way to the byline, he would always curl the ball high and in the air to the far post, where Dillon would be waiting to meet it with a bullet header.

That's how they had scored so many goals. They stuck to the plan. To other teams it looked as if Jamie and Dillon had some kind of telepathic understanding. They didn't. They just knew what was going to happen before their opponents did.

Jamie used the instep of his right boot to sweep the ball smoothly into the near post, where Dillon raced on to it and, first time, buried it high into the roof of the net.

He and Jamie came together by the Bester City goal and conducted their now-familiar celebration. No smiles, no hugs and absolutely no handshakes – there would never be a handshake. Just a solemn-looking high five.

They may not have been close friends or even on speaking terms, but in this league, with Seaport now winning practically every game they played, the pair of them were virtually unstoppable.

Seaport Town 1 - 0 Bester City
D Simmonds, 35

Jamie could see that the Bester players' heads had dropped. He knew that now was the time to attack. One more goal and the game would be over. Bester didn't have the mental strength to come back from two goals down.

Jamie called for the ball as soon as Seaport won it back and, as he took possession, he injected a serious amount of pace into his running. He put his foot on the gas and accelerated forward. Hitting top speed, he flew down the pitch, eating up the ground with each stride.

As he came face to face with the last defender, Jamie wiggled his hips in different directions. He lurched to the left and then feigned to the right before finally bursting on the inside to head directly towards goal.

The keeper came rushing out, but Jamie was in complete control. He saw everything in slow motion. The goalkeeper's face was anguished as he dived towards the ball at Jamie's feet . . . but Jamie was too quick, shifting the ball out of the way . . . and now, with the keeper committed to dive, his body clattered into Jamie's, knocking him down like the last remaining skittle.

Clear penalty. No doubt about it.

Jamie immediately bounced back up to his feet and picked up the ball.

He was just about to put the ball on the spot and take the penalty when he remembered something that Robbie had told him. And the idea that it had given him. . .

Jamie picked the ball up and walked over to Dillon.

"Here," he said, pushing the ball firmly into Dillon's chest. "You take the penalty."

"What are you talking about?" said Dillon. "You won it."

"Yeah," smiled Jamie, "but you need it more than I do."

It felt good to do something decent. For someone else. He just hoped that Robbie would appreciate this.

"What do you mean 'I need it'?" answered Dillon. "I've already scored."

"I mean for the goal bonus. . . For you and Robbie. . . I know your mum's lef—"

But Dillon had pushed the ball back into Jamie's face before he'd finished talking.

"Get lost, you mug!" fumed Dillon. "Like we need *your* charity! And if you ever talk about my mum again, I'll knock you spark out, you little worm!"

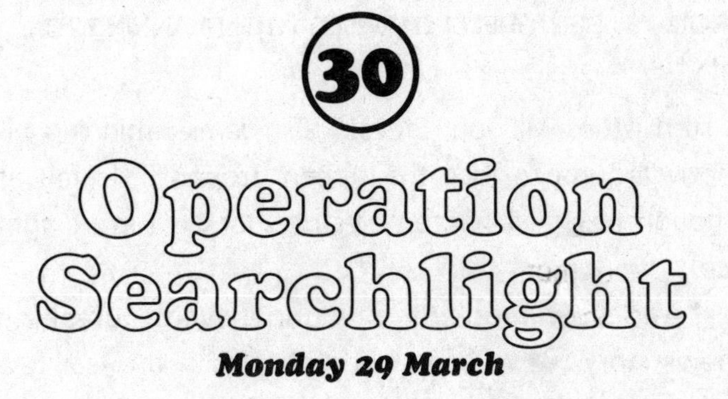

30 Operation Searchlight

Monday 29 March

"Ouuuuch!" yelped Jamie. "You definitely found the pressure point there, Steve! I'm in agony here!"

Jamie was getting a massage on his thigh in the small physio's room at the Seaport training ground. Training had just finished.

"Put on Sports News, will you, Steve, give me something else to think about while you're brutalizing – sorry, fixing – my leg!"

For some reason they weren't showing footy action on the TV. Instead, there were some rather unsteady pictures of a man being bundled into a car. A police car.

It was only then that Jamie registered the scrolling

headline across the bottom of the screen:

BREAKING NEWS . . . MATTHEUS BERTORELLI ARRESTED THIS MORNING . . . POLICE MAKE DAWN RAID . . . BERTORELLI CHARGED WITH PLANNING TO FIX GAME. . .

"Turn it up, will you, Steve!" said Jamie, spinning his body around to face the screen properly. He felt as though he'd just had an electric shock. "Turn it right up!"

"And now more on the unbelievable breaking news story we've been bringing you in the last few minutes. And that news is that Mattheus Bertorelli, the Hawkstone United winger, has been arrested this morning . . . and I'm just hearing that we can now go live to police headquarters, where we believe Detective Colin Hutchence is about to read a short statement. . ."

"At five-thirty this morning, following a tip-off from an anonymous source, an elite police unit raided the home of footballer Mattheus Bertorelli," said the policeman, looking gravely into the camera.

"This unit, code-named Operation Searchlight, had for the last fourteen months been investigating and compiling a dossier into suspected match-fixing within football.

"In Mr Bertorelli's house and on his phone, they

found detailed evidence of a plan to fix a forthcoming high-profile game, alongside arrangements to make millions of pounds through illegal betting on the outcome of this match.

"We believe that Mr Bertorelli himself has significant gambling debts and was being blackmailed by those organizing this plot. However, he is still likely to face a prison term for his involvement.

"We will also take into account the fact that Mr Bertorelli has provided us with the names of all the individuals who were orchestrating this plot. These suspects are currently being arrested and held for questioning.

"So, although the fight against crime continues, today is a significant victory for justice and a great day for the game of football."

As Jamie listened to the words and watched the stream of images on the TV, at first his mind struggled to cope with it all. Then it sank in. Hawkstone were in the clear! He started to grin.

The words "justice" and "great day for football" began to echo in Jamie's ears. A rush of pure pride went through him. *The truth*, Jamie thought to himself. *Finally, now people will know the truth*.

Jamie reached for his phone. He knew exactly who he had to thank—

"Jamie! Jamie!" Stuart Cribbins was suddenly shouting as he sprinted into the physio's room.

"One minute, Stu," Jamie said, scrolling down to Jack's number. "I've just got to make a quick call."

"It's not me, Jamie," insisted Cribbins. "It's Mr Porlock. Says he wants to see you in his office. Now!"

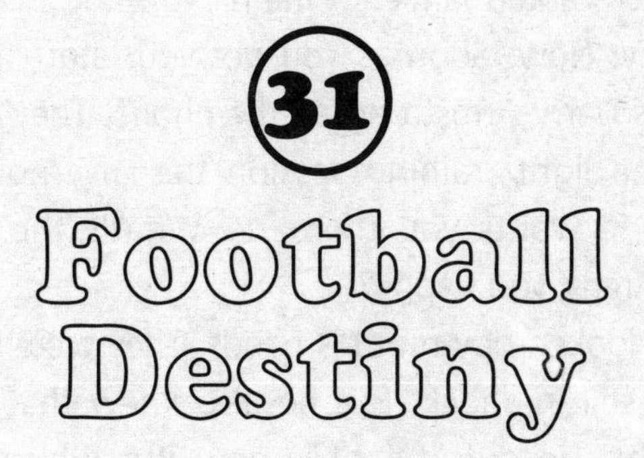

31 Football Destiny

Jamie walked into Raymond Porlock's office to find him on the phone. He had Sports News on the TV too and a serious expression was painted on his face.

"Yes, he's here now," Porlock was saying. "He's just come in."

Then Porlock listened for a few seconds, nodded his head and said: "Sure, I'll tell him," before softly replacing the handset.

Jamie felt his muscles tighten. Was he in trouble? Did the police want to speak to him too? What had Bertorelli told them?

"Sit down, James," said Raymond Porlock, keeping

his eyes fixed on Jamie as he nervously took a seat.

"I've got some good news," Porlock opened. "You're going back to Hawkstone."

"What?" asked Jamie. "When?"

"Today. Now. Soon as you get your stuff together. That was Harry Armstrong on the phone. They're going to have a light training session this afternoon. Set-pieces. He wants you there. . . What's the matter, Jamie? Aren't you happy?"

Jamie looked down at his hands. They were shaking. He was still in shock. But he also knew that Porlock was right; he didn't feel happy. But why not? He should have been jumping up and down with joy at the prospect of going back to Hawkstone. This was what he'd been working towards for the last three months. And now it was here.

"I dunno . . . it's just all so quick, isn't it? It's like one minute I'm here, and the next—"

"Look at the TV, James! It's just like you said – everything! So not only have you done something great for the game, but now, without Bertorelli, Hawkstone need you more than ever. You're going back to the Premier League, son. Where you belong."

"Yeah," Jamie smiled weakly. "I suppose I am . . . it's just . . . you know, this kind of feels like home now, that's all. . ."

And then suddenly an idea rushed into Jamie's mind. A brilliant idea.

"But what if I stayed?!" he asked, jumping out of his chair. "If I stayed with Seaport, we could get promoted through the play-offs this season. I know we could . . . and then one more promotion and we'd all be in the Premier League, together! Imagine it! Seaport Town in the Premier League! We can do it, Mr Porlock! Then I can go back to Hawkstone when I've finished my job here!"

But Raymond Porlock's expression did not reflect Jamie's excitement.

"Now who's the crazy one?" said Porlock, shaking his head.

"What do you mean?" said Jamie. "What are you talking about?"

"You thought I was crazy when you arrived here, didn't you, James?" laughed Porlock. "Go on, you can admit it."

"No, Mr Porlock," Jamie lied. "Of course not."

"Oh, James, come on, it was written all over your face the day you walked into this football club. I could see what you were thinking: *What am I doing here at Seaport Town, being managed by this madman?!*"

Jamie looked down at the floor. He could remember when he'd first stepped into this office and heard the rats scurrying under the floorboards.

"It's all right, James," Porlock laughed. "Don't worry – you wouldn't be the first! I know what they say about me – *mad as a box of frogs* and all that. And anyway, maybe they're right, maybe I am a bit crazy sometimes . . . maybe I am one or two players short of a full team. That's what happens when you've been married to this game for as long as I have.

"Anyway . . . let me tell you something that I *do* know for sure. Very few of us have got a special talent. A reason to be here, if you know what I mean. A promise that we need to fulfil."

Porlock stood up straight. He looked taller than before. Then he walked around his desk and stood next to Jamie.

"You've got that talent, James Johnson," he said. "Your reason for being on this earth is to play in the Premier League. To entertain people. To make them happy. To make them forget about everything else when they watch you play football. And if you waste that talent, *you* would be the real crazy one around here, not me."

Jamie closed his eyes and replayed Porlock's words in his head. Porlock was right. Jamie had a football destiny to fulfil and it wasn't here at Seaport.

He stood up and looked at his manager.

"Thanks for everything, Mr Porlock," said Jamie. "I won't forget you."

Porlock smiled.

"Call me Ray."

32 Good to be Back

"There's something I need to say to you, Jamie," said a solemn-looking Harry Armstrong.

Archie Fairclough had been outside the Hawkstone training ground, waiting for Jamie to arrive. He'd given Jamie a massive bear hug and then led him straight to see the manager.

Now Jamie was staring deep into Harry Armstrong's eyes. Normally Armstrong's sharp eyes reminded Jamie of a shark. They were predatory – as if he might bite off a lump of your flesh at any moment. But now his features appeared softer, gentler.

"I misjudged you, Jamie," Armstrong admitted. "I

misjudged the whole situation. I took the easy option. I believed what I wanted to believe, not what I should have believed. And for that, I am very sorry. Very sorry indeed. But I guess I'm learning just like the rest of us. And I hope you can accept my apology and play for me again."

Jamie looked at Harry Armstrong and smiled. He felt as though a thousand tonnes of pressure had just been lifted from his shoulders. He felt like a Hawkstone player again.

"It's just good to be back," smiled Jamie

"Good to have you here and, if you're happy, I'm going to put you straight back into the team on Saturday. I've watched the DVDs of your last few games at Seaport. Exactly what I was hoping for. You look like you're right back to your best."

"Even better than before!" laughed Jamie. "Maybe it's like they say: everything happens for a reason."

"Good," said Harry. "Because right now I need you – this club needs you – more than it has ever done. And I still believe that we can win this league, by the way."

"So do I, Harry," said Jamie, the adrenaline beginning to pulse around his body like an electric current. "So do I. . ."

Saturday 3 April

Premier League Table

Teams	P	GD	Points
1. Foxborough	30	+41	69
2. Crayhall	31	+31	65
3. Hawkstone United	31	+34	64

Jamie picked up the Hawkstone United shirt. He turned it around and traced his fingers down the material that made up his number. Number 11.

Then, very slowly, relishing every second, Jamie slipped the shirt over his head and on to his shoulders.

Almost without warning, a story that his granddad had read to him when he was younger edged its way into his consciousness. What was it called? *The Sword in the . . . Stone*, that was it – a story about how many men had attempted to remove a special, magical sword from a stone, but there was only one person who could do it, who was destined to do it, because the sword was rightfully his.

Jamie believed that the same principle applied to his Hawkstone United shirt. Many others could try to put it on. They could even wear it. But none of them would ever be able to fill it like Jamie Johnson.

The number 11 shirt of Hawkstone United would always be his. It was his destiny.

He pulled the shirt to his lips and kissed the badge.

He was ready.

Lesterfield City 0 – 0 Hawkstone United
31 MINS PLAYED

Jamie had taken a little while to readjust to playing in the Premier League.

The pace, the skill level, the quality of the defending. He was just a fraction off. But not much.

It felt strange being back on the left wing, not using his right foot as much. It even felt slightly weird not having Dillon's big, bustling figure causing havoc in the opposition penalty area. He wasn't . . . surely not . . . Jamie wasn't actually missing Dillon Simmonds, was he? No. That was out of the question. It was like missing chicken pox. Not possible.

Jamie knew he was back where he belonged, though. Every time he touched the ball, the Hawkstone fans cheered loud and hard. He had even heard some of them shout, "Welcome back – we missed you!" to him during the warm-up.

Jamie could feel something special start to bubble in his blood . . . that sensation he got when his football power coursed through his veins. It told him that he was about to take control of a match.

As Glenn Richardson swivelled majestically in the centre circle, Jamie instinctively set off through the middle. He burst forward like a greyhound chasing a rabbit. If he and Glenn both timed the move right, Jamie's pace would destroy the offside trap.

Richardson spotted Jamie's run and laid a beautiful throughball into his path. The delivery was inch-perfect. Jamie didn't have to break his stride or even take a touch to control . . . he simply belted the ball as hard as he could towards the goal.

The contact was sweet and powerful. The ball flew forward, soaring through the air faster than the human eye could follow.

The ball had ripped into the back of the net before anyone on the pitch or in the stands could move.

Lesterfield City 0 – 1 Hawkstone United
J Johnson, 32

And now Jamie turned and started running.

Running past his teammates . . . past the referee . . . all the way to the other end of the ground. He was going to celebrate with the Hawkstone United fans!

He slid on his knees right to the edge of the pitch.

Then he got up and high fived every Hawkstone fan on the front row of seats. As he put his head in their sea of hands and they patted, hugged and kissed him, a torrent of emotions was being born, or perhaps reborn, within Jamie.

Excitement at being back. Yes – lots of it. Ecstasy at having scored a goal. Of course – by the barrel-load. But there was something else too. Something from deeper inside.

It was pride. Pride at pulling on the Hawkstone shirt once more. Pride at proving all the doubters wrong. And most of all, pride at being himself.

At being Jamie Johnson. Once more.

33
April's
Headlines

JOHNSON
RETURNS
Wing Wizard
Returns
JOHNSON PUTS HAWKSTONE
BACK IN LEAGUE RACE
Hawks Soar on Johnson's Wings
PROFILE: THE FALL AND
RISE OF JAMIE JOHNSON
HAWKSTONE OR
FOXBOROUGH?
WHERE WILL THE
TITLE GO?
Climax to the Premier League
season sees both sides still
vying for the ultimate glory.

Premier League Table - 26 April
FIVE GAMES TO GO

Teams	P	GD	Points
1. Foxborough	33	+45	73
2. Hawkstone United	33	+39	70
3. Larchester Rangers	33	+34	69
4. Crayhall	33	+32	69
5. Brockburn Rovers	33	+20	68
6. Lesterfield City	33	+22	67

34 The Spotlight

Friday 14 May – Two days before the last matches of the season

Jamie was almost blinded by the flashbulbs as he walked into the press room and sat down at the table. There was a jug of water in front of him, and behind him was an advertising board with all of Hawkstone's sponsors. Apparently this press conference was going out all over the world.

Harry Armstrong had said that Jamie didn't have to do it – that the biggest priority was keeping his mind a hundred per cent focused on Sunday's game – but

Jamie had said that he wanted to speak at the press conference. That he had some things he needed to say.

Jamie searched the room to see if he could find Jack. He could spot her instantly in any crowd – it was a kind of sixth sense he had about her. But she wasn't there today. . . At college, no doubt.

"So, Jamie," began one of the journalists. "You and Hawkstone United are right up there and in with a shot of winning the Premier League. I bet you didn't imagine this scenario a few months ago when you were down on loan at Seaport."

Jamie smiled.

"No, I suppose you're right," he said. "And I have to admit that, in the beginning, it was difficult down there . . . but I learned a lot and made some good friends too. I'll be as nervous as anything tonight when I watch them on TV. If they can get into the play-offs, it'll be fantastic for the club."

"What do you think about Mattheus Bertorelli being arrested, Jamie?" asked another journalist. "And can you comment on the rumours that you two had a big bust-up?"

"Er, Jamie does not have to answer that question," said Mark Buttersworth, Hawkstone's media officer. "The Bertorelli case is currently in the hands of the police, so—"

"No, Mark, it's OK," said Jamie, gently. "There is something I want to say about this. It's important to me. I grew up a couple of miles away from here . . . still live in the same house now . . . and I used to walk to this ground with my granddad, who also used to play for Hawkstone, by the way. Football is what I live for. And the way I see it, I just think it's important that we all do whatever we can to protect this game . . . because it's the best game in the world. . ."

After Jamie had finished speaking, there was a second or two of silence, and then all the journalists began writing furiously in their notepads.

"And by the way," Jamie said with a knowing smile. "Whoever the *anonymous source* was who prevented this thing from happening deserves a serious thank-you – from all of us."

Jamie was just getting his phone out to call Jack to see if she'd heard what he'd said when a fat man pushed his way past all the other journalists and poked a voice recorder right under his Jamie's chin.

"Barry Digmore," said the man. "From the *Mercury*. Give me a couple of words about the big game tomorrow," he ordered.

Jamie stared at Barry Digmore. His face was as red as a strawberry and he had blue veins poking out from the side of his nose. His tie was decorated with a variety of crusty stains, and he had a hundred specks of white saliva resting on his rubbery bottom lip.

So you're the one who prints my dad's lies, Jamie thought to himself as he glared at Barry Digmore. *You're the one who judges me. And now you want me to speak to you . . . you want "a couple of words" from me?!*

"Yeah, sure you can have a couple of words," said Jamie, drawing himself up to his full height so he could look down at Digmore's fat, filthy plate of a face.

"Barry Digmore's a LOSER!"

There were a few gasps from the other journalists who were huddled around Jamie. But Jamie didn't care. He'd waited a long time for this moment.

"OK, that's probably enough," said Mark Buttersworth, sweeping his arm protectively around Jamie. "You need to stop now."

Then Mark turned and smiled apologetically to Digmore, saying, "Jamie's under a lot of pressure. Sunday's such a big game. . ."

"No!" said Jamie, freeing himself from Mark's arm. "I'm not stressed at all! I know exactly what I'm saying."

As Mark and Jamie exited the room, Jamie could see out of the corner of his eye that all the other journalists were now laughing at Digmore, mocking him. He could see the anger and embarrassment leaping out from Digmore's oily face.

And although one half of Jamie's brain was worried that he might have gone too far, the other half was shouting: *Serves you right, Barry Digmore! How does it feel to get a taste of your own medicine?*

35 Shouting Technique

Saturday 15 May – The last weekend of the football season

It was as though Jamie was playing in the game himself.

He couldn't stand still. He was jumping up and down and running around the room.

He was watching Seaport Town play. The game was being shown live on TV because, if they won, they would go into the play-offs.

Now the camera was focusing in on Raymond Porlock, who was bellowing instructions from the sidelines. His voice was so loud that you could even hear it on the TV!

"There's no bloomin' grass in the sky!" he was yelling. "So keep the ball on the ground!"

Jamie laughed. He thought back to the time when, one day after training at Seaport, as he was leaving, he'd seen Porlock standing by the side of one of the pitches shouting at the very top of his voice.

"PUSH UP!" he was yelling. "COOONCENTRATE!!!!"

But when Jamie had looked out on to the pitch, he'd seen that no one was there. The entire pitch was empty.

Had Porlock really gone round the bend this time? Jamie had wondered. Had he gone as mad as sixty boxes of frogs all put together?

"Mr Porlock!" Jamie had said to him. "Who are you shouting at? There's no one there!"

Porlock had pretended to look shocked at first, and then he'd smiled at Jamie.

"When you step out over the white line, James, I'm pretty much helpless," he'd said. "There's only one way that I can affect a match while it's happening – and that's by shouting at you lot! Telling you what to do! But shouting is like anything else; there's a technique to it . . . and what I'm doing now is practising that technique."

"So . . . you're . . . practising shouting?"

"Got it in two, James!"

*

Now, on the TV, Seaport were attacking! Dillon Simmonds had laid the ball off to Stuart Cribbins, who was racing through . . . Cribbins was one on one. . . He drilled the ball towards the goal and it beat the goalkeeper . . . but then hit the post!

But that was not it! The ball rebounded so hard that it smashed Stuart Cribbins flat in the face and then bounced back into the goal!

"Ohhhh! You little beauty!" Jamie roared, sprinting around his room in circles like someone doing a rain dance. "Go on, Stuey Cribbins, my son! Smash it in with your face, why don't you! Don't matter how they go in as long as they go in!"

Jamie couldn't wipe the smile from his face.

Seaport Town had made just it in to the play-offs!

On the TV, Jamie could see the whole squad huddled in the centre circle celebrating. Their pride and passion shone out.

It was funny, Jamie thought to himself, how football teams reflected the spirit of their manager. Jamie knew now that he had misjudged Raymond Porlock when he'd first arrived at Seaport. He'd thought that Porlock was mad. He wasn't. He was just mad about football. . .

Jamie's phone started ringing.

He looked at the name flashing up on his screen and he smiled.

He let it ring a couple more times – didn't want to look too eager – and then he answered it just before it was about to go to voicemail.

"Hey," he said.

"JJ!" said Jack. "Thank you! Thank you! Thank you!"

"What for?" asked Jamie.

"For what you said at the press conference today, stupid! The editor at the paper worked out that it was me who tipped off the police! Now they want me to write a massive article for them AND they've asked me to go and work there full-time when I finish my A levels! I'm so excited! I'm going to be a proper journalist! Thank you, JJ!"

"I didn't do anything, Jack," said Jamie. "You're the one who did all the hard work! And you still haven't told me how you did it! You know you're amazing, Jack?"

"Don't be so cheesy!" snapped Jack. She always told Jamie when he overstepped the mark. "Oh, all right, then. Go on, you can be cheesy. Just this once!"

And then they laughed. They had always made each other laugh like this, right back to when Jamie used to sing and make fart noises by putting his hand under his armpit and squeezing it up and down like a bagpipe!

"No, I mean it," insisted Jamie. "If you hadn't

believed me – trusted me – about Bertorelli and then done all that digging . . . well . . . I don't know . . . I guess I'd still be at Seaport and he'd still be—"

"Hey, don't sweat it, Jamie. What are friends for, right?"

"Right," said Jamie.

And then a silence fell down the phone line. It sat there, waiting. . .

"Jack?" There was a stammer in Jamie's voice and his stomach was beginning to ache.

"Yeah?"

What are you worried about? Jamie asked himself. *Just get on with it!*

"No . . . it's nothing . . . don't worry about it. . ."

Coward! Why am I such a coward?!

"Come on, Jamie . . . spit it out, will you?"

"No . . . I was just wondering if . . . after the game tomorrow . . . I didn't know whether you wanted to . . . I dunno . . . maybe we could—"

"You can pick me up at eight," said Jack, putting Jamie out of his misery. "*If* you do the business for the Hawks tomorrow!"

And then she was gone. Jack was never a great one for goodbyes.

Jamie looked at his phone and shook his head. How was it she always knew what he was thinking?

Sunday 16 May – Final matches of the Premier League Season

Premier League Table
WITH ONE MATCH TO PLAY

Teams	P	GD	Points
1. Foxborough	37	+51	79
2. Hawkstone United	37	+44	79

Foxborough v Liverton
Hawkstone v Brockburn Rovers
MATCHES KICK OFF AT 16.00

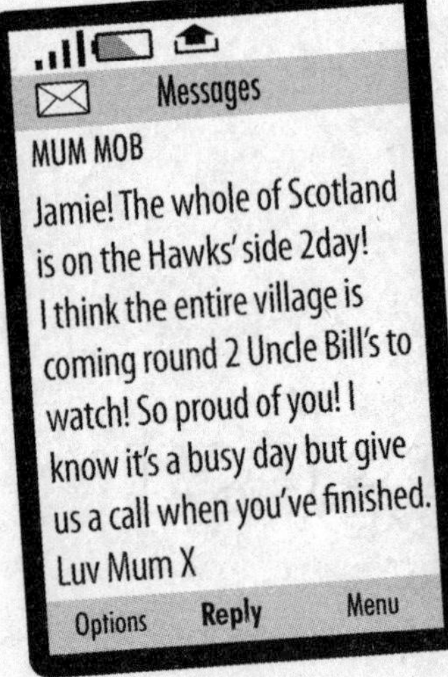

Jamie put his phone back in his pocket. That text would have made his granddad, Mike, so proud.

In many ways, Jamie felt as though his football career was for Mike as much as for himself. Jamie had got all his talent from Mike so now it was his job to make the most of that talent.

Jamie would be playing for both of them today.

Jamie looked out of the car window at all the kids pressed up against the glass. They had been waiting outside his house since this morning, just trying to catch a glimpse of him.

And now, as he was leaving to head to the ground, they were there to see him off. As Doug started up the engine, Jamie suddenly had a flashback to when he had been one of those kids. He remembered how excited he'd been whenever he'd seen a real footballer, live in the flesh.

"Just hang on for a minute, will you, Doug?" Jamie said. "I'll be back in a sec."

Then Jamie Johnson got back out of the car.

The kids let out a cheer and gathered around him as though he were the Pied Piper.

"Score a goal for us today, Jamie!" they said.

"Are you going to win the league for us?" they asked.

"Can we have your shirt after the game?!" they joked.

Jamie signed every single one of their autographs. He knew that the next Jamie Johnson was in there somewhere.

"Are you ready to go?" Doug asked Jamie as he got back in the car.

Jamie closed his eyes and breathed in deeply. Today was the day of all days. Hawkstone United's chance to win the Premier League.

"As ready as I'll ever be."

"Let's have a look at the paper," Jamie said to Archie Fairclough while he was getting a massage to loosen his muscles ahead of the game.

Archie shifted around uncomfortably on his feet.

"Papers ain't come in today, Jamie," he said. "Postal strike or something."

"Archie, I'm a pretty bad liar – but you must be the worst liar in the world!" laughed Jamie. "You can't even look me in the eye! Come on, give it here! I know

The Mercury, Sunday 16 May

SPORTS NEWS

JOHNSON CRACKS UP ON THE EVE OF THE BIGGEST MATCH OF HIS LIFE!

Title Decider Special – Foxborough & Hawkstone Fight for the Right to be Premier League Champions!

BARRY DIGMORE GIVES IT TO YOU STRAIGHT

Hawkstone United's star player, Jamie Johnson, showed that the pressure is really getting to him as he prepares for today's title showdown.

Just hours before the biggest match of his life, Jamie Johnson **LOST IT** during yesterday's press conference, launching a completely unprovoked verbal attack on **ME** for simply doing my job! When I asked him a simple question about how he was feeling ahead of today's titanic clash, Johnson lost the plot completely, hurling a series of insults at me. Clearly, at only seventeen, the pressure of competing for the Premier League title is too much for this **BOY**.

Today may be the biggest match in Hawkstone's history, but I predict it will be Foxborough that take the title, with Jamie Johnson revealed to be nothing more than the weak-minded **ONE-TRICK PONY** that he is.

What do you think? Have you ever seen a top star crack up and lose the plot? Who do you think will win the Premier League – Hawkstone or Foxborough? Is Jamie Johnson a ***ONE-TRICK PONY****? Tell Barry and earn yourself some cash!*

digthedirt@digmore.com

it's a big game, but I'm not nervous. I promise."

"Gaffer's orders," explained Archie, holding his ground. "You're not supposed to look at the papers."

"Archie, either *you* give me the paper or I go outside and get one off the fans. Your call. . ."

Archie considered his options for a couple of moments and then, with extreme reluctance, handed Jamie the newspaper.

"Thank you," said Jamie, a little sarcastically. Then, instinctively, he turned the paper over to read the back page.

"What's he doing reading that rubbish?!" shouted Harry Amstrong, storming into the massage room and ripping the paper out of Jamie's stunned hands. "I told you not to let him read it – under *any* circumstances!"

But it was too late.

Jamie had read every word.

Playing for the Title

"OK, Gary," said the producer into the presenter's ear. "We're live in 3 . . . 2 . . . 1. . . You're on the air. . ."

"So welcome to our very special coverage of this, the final day of the Premier League season. Now for those of you who have been living on another planet, let me remind you of the situation at the top of the table: Hawkstone and Foxborough are level on points. Foxborough hold the potentially all-important advantage of a better goal-difference. Which all means that Hawkstone must simply get a better result than Foxborough today to win the Premier League Title. . .

"We'll be switching live between both games to keep

you right up to date with all the action, and joining us here in the studio to enjoy the afternoon with us, we welcome one of the real characters of the game . . . Raymond Porlock.

"So, Raymond, how do you see today's events unfolding?"

"Too close for me to call, I'm afraid. . . But I will tell you one, thing, Gary: sometimes football can be the simplest game in the world. In the end, today might just come down to which team actually wants it more."

Down in the tunnel, waiting to walk out on to the pitch, Jamie Johnson was doing everything he could to relax: concentrating on taking deep breaths . . . trying to clear his mind of everything other than winning the League title for Hawkstone United.

"Eh, good luck, mate! See you out there, yeah?"

It was the Brockburn Rovers' young full-back, Ashley Blake, shaking Jamie's hand. Blake, like Jamie, was seventeen years old and was being hailed as the best young full-back in the country. He'd only been playing football for the last seven years. Before that he'd been a hundred-metre sprinter. He still held the schools' record. You could see it in his calf muscles. They were huge.

Blake was Jamie's direct opponent today. So why was he being so nice? And why was he smiling so much?

Wasn't he scared of facing Jamie?

But there was no time to think about anything else.

It was 3.55 p.m. The players from both sides stared straight ahead as they walked out of the tunnel. There was a loud pop song playing, but it was completely drowned out by the gigantic blast of noise from the Hawkstone fans when they saw the players emerge. The sound – like a volcano erupting – rushed into Jamie's ears.

It told him that this was going to be like no other game he had played in his life.

39 Kick-Off!

Hawkstone United v Brockburn Rovers
16.00 KICK-OFF

As Brockburn got the game under way, Jamie looked around the ground. Almost every fan had brought a flag or banner. And most had his name on them:

JAMIE J – HE'LL BRING THE LEAGUE OUR WAY!

JJ – FASTEST PLAYER IN THE WORLD!

JAMIE JOHNSON IS HAWKSTONE UNITED

As soon as Hawkstone won possession, they immediately swept the ball out to the left to find Jamie, just as they had been instructed to do in every game since he had returned.

Jamie had the ball at his feet – and then suddenly the whole ground went quiet. All eyes were on the action. All eyes on Jamie . . . waiting. . .

The fans who had worked all week to have enough money to come and watch this massive game – they were all here to watch Jamie. To see some magic flow from his boots. To see him deliver.

Play your normal game, Jamie ordered himself. *They're not here to put pressure on you – they're here to support you! Go for it!*

Jamie knocked the ball down the line past Ashley Blake and raced off after it at maximum speed. But then something happened that had never occurred before: Jamie got to the ball second! In a straight foot race, he had been beaten to the ball.

Ashley Blake was faster than Jamie Johnson!

Blake knocked the ball out easily for a throw-in and then turned, smiling, almost laughing, towards Jamie.

"Is that all you've got?" he smirked, chucking the ball to Jamie to take the throw-in. "I heard you were quick."

"Mate," said Jamie, pretending to be unaffected, "I haven't even started yet!"

But inside Jamie felt sick. His whole body was

squirming. He could feel a weakness invading his veins.

This had never happened before, and he didn't know how to deal with it. In his entire life, he'd never come up against anyone who was as fast as he was.

The next time Jamie received the ball – this time from a delicate Rigobert West chip down the line – he went for it again. If he could just find his turbo gear, maybe he could still beat Blake. This time he really turned on the afterburners, gave it everything he'd got.

But he just couldn't get away from Blake. The defender stayed with him, neck and neck, before sliding in to nick possession from Jamie with a perfectly timed challenge. He even kept the ball too. Jamie could see the grin on Blake's face as he sprinted forward out of defence.

"Come on, Jamie," the Hawkstone fans were shouting, almost begging him. "Don't flop now! We need you, mate. Foxborough have just taken the lead in their game!"

16.27 – Score Updates

SCORE AT FOXBOROUGH
Foxborough 1 - 0 Liverton
L O'Kane, 26

SCORE AT HAWKSTONE
Hawkstone United 0 - 0 Brockburn Rovers

Projected Premier League Table (if scores stay the same)

Teams	P	GD	Points
1. Foxborough	38	+52	82
2. Hawkstone United	38	+44	80

Jamie's heart sank. There was a long way to go, but everyone knew that if Foxborough won their game, there was no way Hawkstone could take the league.

Jamie sprinted infield in search of the ball. But everywhere he went, Ashley Blake followed. It was as though Blake had taken him prisoner and Jamie had no way of finding the key to set himself free.

As it became increasingly obvious that Blake had Jamie in his pocket, the Brockburn fans began taunting Jamie.

Soon, they were in full voice, mocking Jamie with Barry Digmore's criticism from today's paper: "One-trick pony, he's just a one-trick ponyyy!"

Jamie was angry. He could feel his temples pulsating as he fumed at his own inability to get the better of Blake.

It was only now that he realized how much he had always relied on his pace. It was his super power. His way of always beating his man. But now that had been taken away from him.

Jamie could only look on, helpless, when right on the cusp of half-time, the Brockburn centre forward belted a volley towards goal from twenty yards out. It was a great strike, but it didn't go in.

It hit the crossbar. But then the rebound smacked into the back of the Hawkstone goalkeeper's head and bounced in.

It was a horrible, ugly goal. The Hawkstone crowd had been silenced. Their hopes extinguished. They looked to Jamie. Prayed for him to do something. But Jamie had no idea how to bring back the magic.

16.44 – Score Updates

SCORE AT FOXBOROUGH
Foxborough 1 - 0 Liverton
L O'Kane, 26

SCORE AT HAWKSTONE
Hawkstone United 0 - 1 Brockburn Rovers
E Fishlock (O.G), 44

Projected Premier League Table
(if scores stay the same)

Teams	P	GD	Points
1. Foxborough	38	+52	82
2. Hawkstone United	38	+43	79

40 Make History

HALF-TIME

It was a boiling-hot day and the results were going exactly the wrong way for Hawkstone, but Harry Armstrong still looked like the coolest man in the ground.

He was wearing a brand new grey suit and there was not a crease on it.

He stood in front of his players in the Hawkstone United dressing room, staring each one of them dead in the eye. Jamie could see that his manager's shark eyes had returned.

It reminded Jamie of the occasion when Harry Armstrong had been playing for Hawkstone and there had been a ruck during a match against Crayhall. He'd taken on *three* of their team – and dealt with all of them. He'd been given a four-match ban for his troubles, but after that day, everyone in football knew never to mess with Harry Armstrong.

Armstrong was a warrior and his troops were waiting for him to unleash his fury on them. Would he pin them up against the wall and shout in their faces? Would he fling a tray of teacups across the room to frighten them into action? Harry Armstrong was capable of anything. . .

But instead, for two whole minutes, he said absolutely nothing. His stare was more than threatening enough.

Then, finally, he spoke.

"How dare you drop your heads?" he began. He wasn't shouting, though. He didn't have to. The fact that his voice was so calm and measured somehow made him even more scary than if he had been hollering wildly.

"How dare you give me that look like this title race is over? You . . . every single one of you . . . have the chance to make history today. This football club has never won the league, and here you lot are, potentially forty-five minutes away from achieving it, and you look like you've already been beaten.

"I want you to imagine for just a second what it

will be like if we do this today. If we really make this happen. Have you any idea what it will mean to those fans? And to you lot? They won't just be talking about this team for the next week or couple of months . . . they will remember you for decades. . .

"In sixty years' time, kids who are up there in the stands today will be grandparents, and they will be telling their grandkids about the day that Hawkstone United won the Premier League for the first time. Now, do you lot want to sit here accepting defeat before it's happened, or shall we go out there and make history?"

"Boss," said Jamie as the players were heading out for the second half. "Have you thought about swapping me over to the right side? It's where I played at Seaport and it worked really we—"

"Archie!" called Harry Armstrong, cutting Jamie off in mid-flow. "Have a word with your mate, will you . . . dispense some wisdom for me – we've got a match to win."

Archie Fairclough strode over and put his arm around Jamie.

"Let me tell you something very quickly, Jamie," he said. "When you go out there on to that pitch, it's not about you versus Ashley Blake. Got nothing to do with that. You've got enough talent in your little finger to beat any defender. It's about you understanding how good you are. Once you do that, everything else will fall into place, trust me."

"Thanks, Archie," said Jamie. Sometimes Archie reminded Jamie of his granddad, Mike. They both believed in him. No matter what.

"Just take your time, Jamie," smiled Archie. "You'll work out it . . . you always do."

Then Archie put his hand behind Jamie's back and gave him an almighty shove, practically throwing him back out on to the pitch!

"Now go out there and make yourself a bloomin' legend!"

41

Feeling the Heat

"And we cross over immediately to The Lair, where Foxborough are taking on Liverton. There's been a very early goal in the second half . . . Hawkstone fans, listen up!"

"Yes . . . thanks, Gary, you join us here where Foxborough have just conceded! It's now one to one!"

17.03 – Score Updates

SCORE AT FOXBOROUGH
Foxborough 1 - 1 Liverton
L O'Kane, 26 H Rodinaldo, 47

SCORE AT HAWKSTONE

Hawkstone United 0 - 1 Brockburn Rovers

E Fishlock (O.G.), 44

Projected Premier League Table
(if scores stay the same)

Teams	P	GD	Points
1. Foxborough	38	+51	80
2. Hawkstone United	38	+43	79

"Hugo Rodinaldo could have just done Hawkstone United a huge favour! So, with this game all even, it's now back in Hawkstone's hands! If they can find a way to come back and beat Brockburn, they win the leag – but hang on! Stay with us here, as now Foxborough are back on the attack! They've got a two against one . . . surely . . . it must be . . . it ISSSSSSSSSS!

"Foxborough go back into the lead! That's what champions are made of!"

17.05 – Score Updates

SCORE AT FOXBOROUGH

Foxborough 2 - 1 Liverton

L O'Kane, 26 H Rodinaldo, 47

D Rouzel, 49

SCORE AT HAWKSTONE
Hawkstone United 0 - 1 Brockburn Rovers
E Fishlock (O.G.), 44

Projected Premier League Table
(if scores stay the same)

Teams	P	GD	Points
1. Foxborough	38	+52	82
2. Hawkstone United	38	+43	79

As the drama of the events at Foxborough filtered through, the Hawkstone fans were glued to their radios, jumping up and down, screaming and booing. One fan even fainted. And if they were feeling the heat, so too were the players.

Sweat was running down Jamie's forehead. His heart was beating a thousand times a minute. And he was still getting no change whatsoever out of Ashley Blake.

His mind was a blur of questions. What could he do? How could he turn things around? He would give anything to inspire Hawkstone to victory today, but somehow he felt as though he'd hit a brick wall. . .

"I think I'm going to take him off," said Harry Armstrong to Archie Fairclough. "What do you reckon?"

Archie Fairclough smiled. A big, broad smile.

"You know what I think, Harry. Same as always: I'd never bet against Jamie Johnson."

"Yeah, and normally I'd agree with you, but look at him, Archie. Look at his body language. It's all over the place. His head's gone. He's not right. We have to do something . . . I'm making the change."

Jamie looked at the board. His number was up. Literally. And although his stomach was plummeting through his body, he couldn't argue. Football wasn't about one player; it was about what was best for the whole team. He'd learned that much at Seaport. And while there was still a chance for Hawkstone, they had to take it.

"Substitution for Hawkstone United after seventy-three minutes," said the stadium announcer. "Coming off, number eleven, Jamie Johnson, to be replaced by number twenty-six, Benny Kamara."

Jamie clapped the Hawkstone fans and quickly ran towards the touchline to make way for Kamara.

In fact, he was barely an inch away from leaving the pitch when Archie Fairclough dashed out from the dugout and hurriedly put his hand out to stop Jamie leaving the pitch.

"Wait there!" said Archie to Jamie before turning to Harry Armstrong.

"Harry!" he shouted. "Look at Glenn! He's in trouble!"

They all turned to see that Glenn Richardson was lying on the ground, screaming out in agony. He was holding his knee and calling out for the physio.

"Aaah!" he was shouting. "Heard something snap! Think it's the cruciate!"

42 Lightning Bolt

"I need you to stay on for the moment," said Armstrong, putting his arm around Jamie as they watched Glenn Richardson being stretchered off the pitch. "I just need to work out what I'm going to do."

Both Harry and Jamie tapped Glenn Richardson on the head as he was carried away down the tunnel to the waiting ambulance.

He was in so much pain he'd put a blanket over his face so people couldn't see his eyes. He didn't want them to see the tears.

Play had been stopped for seven minutes to allow him to be treated and stretchered from the field. There hadn't even been anyone near him when the injury had occurred. Richardson had simply caught his studs in the turf as he was turning. It had snapped his cruciate knee ligament: the worst injury in football.

In the break in play, both sets of players had gathered around the dugouts to talk to their managers and get some water on board. It was well past five p.m. now, but the temperature on the pitch was still soaring.

Jamie had so much to think about. So much pressure. He wandered away from the rest of the Hawkstone players in some kind of daze. He didn't really know where he was.

"Hey, Jamie! Jamie!" he heard people shouting from the crowd. They were familiar voices . . . and familiar faces. . .

It was the Seaport squad. All of them!

They must have all come to support him! And they were all wearing their Seaport Town strips. At least now it was warm enough to wear the short-sleeved shirts!

At the front of the group, someone was frantically trying to get his attention.

It was Dillon Simmonds.

"Oi!" he was shouting, loudly. "Oi! Come here!"

Jamie didn't know what to do. The last thing he

needed now was Dillon Simmonds barking insults at him. He was obviously still wound up about Jamie offering him that penalty. But Robbie was there too, and he was also calling Jamie over.

As soon as Jamie got within arm's reach of the crowd, Dillon snaked out his hand and grabbed Jamie's wrist so tightly it practically crushed every single bone.

Before the stewards could intervene, he pulled Jamie towards him and aggressively stared him straight in the face.

"You've got a job to do, mate," he snarled. "The reason you're out on that pitch and I'm in the stands is cos you've got the skill that I never had. Now if you don't start using it, I'm going to get pretty angry. Just play like you did at Seaport, will you? Go and do what you've got to do."

As he took in Dillon's order, a slow realization began to wash over Jamie. And then a sudden lightning bolt of understanding flashed into his mind. . .

But he had to be quick. The referee was blowing his whistle. It was time to get the game back on.

All the Hawkstone players sprinted on to the pitch and back into their positions . . . all except Jamie, who had gone missing.

Then, finally, he reappeared. The last one back on the

pitch. Still tucking his shirt into his shorts.

"Where's he been?" asked Harry Armstrong. "I can still take him off, you know, Archie . . . we've got one more sub."

"Five minutes," said Archie Fairclough. "Just give the boy five more minutes. . ."

Had Archie detected something different in the way Jamie was moving? Had he spotted that familiar glint of confidence returning to Jamie's eyes? Or was he just gambling?

Either way, Harry Armstrong nodded and said: "OK, Archie. Five more minutes."

"Yes!" Jamie roared, as soon as play was back under way. "Play me in!"

Jamie galloped on to the ball and ran at Ashley Blake. Ran hard. But his brain was working even faster. Yes, he knew by now that Blake was as quick as he was on the outside. But there was something he hadn't tried yet. . .

Jamie swivelled, spinning his body around, while at the same time manipulating the ball with the sole of his boot. He did a double drag-back to get a yard ahead of Ashley Blake.

And now he cut inside on to his right foot. He was a little unsteady at first, but there was no time for hesitation. This was the right foot that he'd spent hours working on at Seaport. He had to trust it now . . . trust himself . . . trust his talent. . .

Jamie powered forward into the box. Blake was behind him. The two speed merchants sprinted after the ball, but Jamie's skill had given him a head start.

Jamie knew that this was the moment. He knew exactly what he had to do. He pulled his right foot back and smashed it into the ball, laces first. He followed all the way through, lifting his foot almost head-high after he'd struck the shot, to achieve the maximum power possible.

The effect was devastating. The ball seemed to have the force of ten rockets as it soared at supersonic speed through the air.

It was a goal from the millisecond it left Jamie's boot.

And it was an absolute beauty too. It fairly ripped into the back of the net!

If he'd thought about it, Jamie could have done the robot dance or slid on his knees towards the fans to celebrate. But as soon as he saw the ball go in, Jamie's mind went completely blank and his body came to a standstill.

All he could feel was relief. Hawkstone were back in it. They had lift-off!

17.30 – Score Updates

SCORE AT FOXBOROUGH

Foxborough 2 - 1 Liverton

L O'Kane, 26 H Rodinaldo, 47

D Rouzel, 49

SCORE AT HAWKSTONE

Hawkstone United 1 - 1 Brockburn Rovers

J Johnson, 74 E Fishlock (O.G.), 44

Projected Premier League Table
(if scores stay the same)

Teams	P	GD	Points
1. Foxborough	38	+52	82
2. Hawkstone United	38	+44	80

"How did he do that, Raymond?" asked the TV presenter. "You know him better than us, having managed him this season. We see nothing from him for the whole game and then BANG! A moment of utter genius! Please, Raymond, explain to us the enigma that is Jamie Johnson!"

"That's easy, Gary. On the football pitch, most of us live in the present. James Johnson lives in the fut—"

"I'm sorry, but I'm going to have to interrupt you

straight away there, Raymond, because we are getting some absolutely sensational news coming into us from the other game at the top of the table . . . there's been another goal up at Foxborough and the goal has gone . . . against Foxborough! That's right! Liverton have equalized! All of which means that this League title is now on a knife edge! One more goal for either Foxborough or Hawkstone and the Premier League is theirs!"

17.32 – Score Updates

SCORE AT FOXBOROUGH
Foxborough 2 - 2 Liverton

L O'Kane, 26 | H Rodinaldo, 47
D Rouzel, 49 | B Sharpe, 76

SCORE AT HAWKSTONE
Hawkstone United 1 - 1 Brockburn Rovers

J Johnson, 74 | E Fishlock (O.G.), 44

Projected Premier League Table
(if scores stay the same)

Teams	P	GD	Points
1. Foxborough	38	+51	80
2. Hawkstone United	38	+44	80

As the news reverberated around the Hawkstone ground, the noise reached almost unbearable levels. It seemed as though the old stadium might crumble under the weight of hope and expectation. It was being rocked to its foundations by the jumping sea of excitement inside.

The Hawkstone fans were trying to suck the goal into the back of the Brockburn net. One goal! That was all they needed.

But time was against them.

With three minutes left, Hawkstone won a corner.

"Everybody up!" Harry Armstrong shouted, leaping up from the dugout. "Everybody get in there! Including you, Eddie! Yes, you!"

Every single one of the Hawkstone players sprinted into the Brockburn penalty area, including Eddie Fishlock, the huge American keeper!

Harry Armstrong was gambling. Big time. He knew it was now or never.

In came the corner . . . the ball hanging in the air like a perfectly ripe apple just waiting to be plucked. Fishlock jumped high, getting a vital touch to flick the ball on to the far post.

Everyone in the ground looked on as Rigobert West leapt into the air. The Beast rose majestically. He strained all of his bulging neck muscles and bulleted in a header.

It hit the angle of the crossbar and post.

Then the ball bounced down on to the goal-line.

And there it remained . . . right on the line . . . right next to the goalpost . . . waiting. . .

The two quickest players on the pitch sped towards the ball. If the defender got there first, he'd clear the ball. If the striker won the race, it would be a certain goal.

The race was between Ashley Blake and Jamie Johnson. Whoever won would decide the game.

They both launched themselves at the ball.

And that was all that was in Jamie's mind. Perhaps, somewhere in his brain, he knew that if he got there first, he would also clatter into the goalpost. But if he did know it, he ignored it just the same.

The desire for glory overrode the fear of pain. Winning was all that mattered.

Jamie unleashed everything he had. Found his ultra-turbo gear. Tapped into his unbreakable spirit. . .

He got his foot to the ball first . . . and then smashed his head full pelt into the post.

He was knocked out instantly.

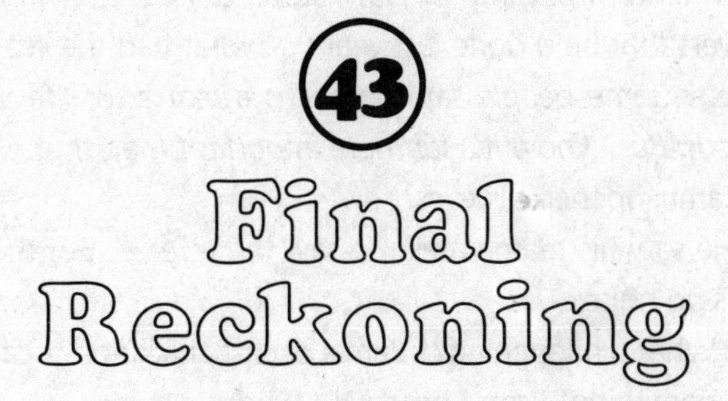

43 Final Reckoning

Jamie Johnson was not moving.

He was still. *Dead* still.

The referee knelt over his prone body and immediately called on the paramedics.

They sprinted over to Jamie and felt his neck and head.

The Hawkstone players all gathered around him.

Jamie had been brave. Unbelievably brave. But had he been reckless too? Had he sacrificed everything, including his career, just to get to that ball first? His body had been damaged before. It might not be able to withstand another serious injury.

In Jamie's semi-conscious mind, old pictures were reappearing: his mum crying after his dad had left them. Kicking a ball with his granddad for the first time. Dreaming of playing for Hawkstone United. . . And the advert that he'd done last year . . . what had the words been? *Some people say football is a matter of life and death. But I know it's far more important than that. . .*

Jamie opened his eyes.

He saw his teammates. He saw the referee. But there was no noise.

"What's happening?" Jamie said, panicking. "I can't hear anything! I can't hear ANYthing!"

And then, like a dam breaking, the noise burst into Jamie's ears. The cheering, the screams, the joy!

It was the Hawkstone fans! All of them!

Celebrating a goal!

"Did it go in?!" Jamie screamed. "Did we do it?!"

He already knew the answer was yes.

17.36 – FULL-TIME

SCORE AT FOXBOROUGH

Foxborough 2 - 2 Liverton

L O'Kane, 26	H Rodinaldo, 47
D Rouzel, 49	B Sharpe, 76

SCORE AT HAWKSTONE

Hawkstone United 2 - 1 Brockburn Rovers

J Johnson, 74, 87 E Fishlock (O.G.), 44

Final Premier League Table

Teams	P	GD	Points
1. Hawkstone United (C)	38	+45	82
2. Foxborough	38	+51	80

Hawkstone United are Premier League Champions for the first time in the club's history!

"Yes! Yes! Yes!" screamed Jamie, as the final whistle went. He was tearing around the pitch, leaping in the air, hugging anyone he could lay his hands on. For a second, he even went to hug the referee too, but managed to stop himself at the very last moment. He'd learned his lesson on that front!

"And so, Raymond," said the presenter. "Now we come to the verdict for your man of the match, please. . ."

"Yes indeed, Gary," Raymond Porlock was saying way up in the commentary gantry, a big, wide grin stretched across his face. "The man of the match has to go to a young man called . . . Rigobert West. Only kidding! But I had you there, Gary my old mucker, didn't I? Come on, admit it! No, in all seriousness, of course the man of the match is Jamie Johnson . . . who else?"

Out on the pitch it was turning into the party of all parties! The Hawks fans were singing, "One Jamie Johnson, there's only one Jamie Johnson!"

It was the song they had first sung to him when he'd scored an overhead kick on the day he'd been Hawkstone's mascot. He had only been eleven years old that day, but his talent had still shone out like a beacon.

Hearing the Hawkstone fans sing his name electrified Jamie's body.

"I love football!" he shouted, jumping high into the air, punching his fist skyward.

By now, the other Hawkstone players were spraying champagne over themselves in the middle of the pitch.

But Jamie left them to it for a minute or two.

He headed over to the crowd. There was one last thing he had to do. . .

Jamie jogged over to the part of the ground where all the Seaport players were. They were celebrating as if *they* had just won the league. There was even a group of fans watching and cheering Stuart Cribbins as he did his robot dance!

Jamie took off his Hawkstone shirt and handed it over to Robbie Simmonds. He'd realized now who it was that Robbie so reminded him of. It had been nagging away at Jamie for weeks. And then suddenly, one morning, the answer had just popped into his head. Robbie reminded Jamie of himself.

"One day," Jamie said to Robbie, handing over his number 11 shirt. "One day, you'll be wearing this shirt. I just know it."

"Course I will, you pumpkin!" said Robbie, snatching the shirt. "As long as you keep coaching me!

"Hey!" Robbie continued, pointing to the blue-and-white-striped football top that Jamie still had on. "Why are you wearing that?!"

Jamie looked down at the short-sleeved Seaport Town shirt that he had hurriedly nicked off Stuart Cribbins at half-time and put on underneath his Hawkstone top . . . minutes before he'd scored the two most important goals of his life.

"Well, your brother told me to play like I did at Seaport . . . thought I'd take his advice," smiled Jamie.

"Nice one, Dillon," said Jamie, reaching out his hand.

Dillon Simmonds didn't say a word. Or crack a smile. He simply grabbed Jamie's hand and shook it. Hard.

44
Time to Lift the Trophy

"Jamie! Over here!"

"Jamie! Just a few words! How do you feel?"

Jamie looked over at the throng of journalists waiting for him, all jostling to speak to him.

Strange, he thought, a *few months ago, none of you wanted to know me. Now you all want a piece of me*.

Jamie looked among their faces. Even old Barry Digmore was there, desperately holding out his voice recorder.

But there was only one person Jamie was looking for in that sea of journalists.

Jamie spotted Jack immediately. She was standing

aside from the other journalists, looking straight at Jamie. She wasn't smiling or trying to get an interview; she was simply pointing at her watch.

Jamie couldn't help laughing. He knew exactly what Jack was thinking: *Make sure you're not late, Jamie . . . I said eight o'clock, remember!*

She needn't have worried. Jamie would never keep Jack waiting.

"Jamie!" shouted Archie Fairclough, his face flushed red with happiness. "Get yourself over here, son! Time to lift the trophy!"

Jamie sprinted over and gave Archie a massive high five, followed by a huge bear hug. He knew that, in Archie, he'd found someone else he could trust.

As he leapt up on to the platform to collect his medal, Jamie felt the ghosts of the last few months finally slip away from him. . .

Being betrayed again by his dad; finding out that Mattheus Bertorelli wasn't a superstar – he was only a cheat; being banished to Seaport Town . . . even questioning whether his whole career was over. All those dark shadows were departing. . .

Jamie wiped the sweat from his hands as he and his teammates edged closer to the prize. And as he drew nearer to the immaculate trophy, which was glistening now in the bright May sunshine, it occurred to Jamie that all of those old ghosts, all those challenges, had been part of the journey. His journey.

Which had led him here.

To exactly where he had always wanted to be.

Jamie roared with a joy that came from deep in his soul as he and his Hawkstone United teammates lifted the Premier League trophy for the first time in their history.

Now music was playing and the Hawkstone team were bouncing around in celebration, each taking their turn to kiss the trophy.

When it came to Jamie's turn, every single Hawkstone fan in the ground rose to their feet to applaud him.

They were his football family. They had seen him grow up. Seen him turn from a boy with limitless potential into the footballer that they had all hoped he would become. And right now, he was living out all their dreams.

They clapped him as a Hawkstone hero. As a Premier League star. And they cheered him as one of their own.

Jamie Johnson was back.

Back where he belonged . . . with the world at his feet.

Interview with Dan Freedman

You've been to the World Cup twice, what was it like?

Before becoming an author, I worked as a journalist with the England Football Team. That meant living in the team hotel, having breakfast with players like Wayne Rooney and Steven Gerrard and then going to watch them train and play in the World Cup Finals. They were some of the greatest experiences of my life. I realize how lucky I was and I thought about those times a lot when I was writing this book.

Can you do all of Jamie's best moves?

Of course I can – I'm a phenomenal footballer, one of the best in the world. See, that's the good thing about being an author: you can just make stuff up.

Who are your favourite footballers at the moment?

You can't ignore Messi's majestic talent and I absolutely love the way that Xavi never ever loses the ball. Gerrard for his passion and loyalty to his club and, for the future, Jack Wilshere. So young but soooo good!

You visit lots of schools – what's the funniest question you've been asked?

Lots of kids seem fascinated to know what car I drive (a Golf, if you must know). Some ask me if I ever get bored of football (no). And one boy asked me which footballer had the biggest appetite when it came to meal times! The school visits are great fun because they are a chance for me to meet the people that I write the books for.

Who is the most famous person you've interviewed?

Take your pick: David Beckham, Cristiano Ronaldo, Sir Alex Ferguson. At the time, I had pretend that it was no big deal and that I was all cool about it but inside I was thinking: "Oh my God! I can't believe I'm interviewing him!"

So have you ever had a kick around with Wayne Rooney?

No – I think I would be too worried about injuring him if I timed a tackle wrong! That would be a disaster! I did once get to play against Demetrio Albertini though. He was one of the best midfielders in the world when I was growing up – he won the Champions League with AC Milan. I played against him in midfield in a friendly game. Would you believe me if I told you we won?!

What inspires you to write these books?

When I was younger I wasn't a massive reader. People used to tell me to read all the time but there were no books out there that excited me. They all seemed boring. The Jamie Johnson series is for people out there who are like I was. I try to write the kind of books that I would have been desperate to read.

What's the best game you've ever been to?

In 2002, I was in Japan for the World Cup quarter-final: Brazil v England. It doesn't get much bigger than that!

Jamie Johnson books are often about triumphing over the odds. Can you give us any tips on how to become a professional footballer?

I think it's about your physical and mental dedication. Are you training as hard as you can? Are you working on your weaker foot? Do you believe in yourself? Are you trying to improve every time you play? And, if you get knocked back, how will you react? If you come back stronger, you've got half a chance.

And the other thing to remember is that even if you don't make it as a professional footballer, there are so many other jobs that you can get which involve football. Doctor, physiotherapist, coach, architect... The possibilities are all there, it's a case of going for your goals.

Want more thrilling footballing action? Catch up on Jamie Johnson's journey to the top.

Jamie Johnson's desperate to become his school's star football player (and in his dreams, a top professional too). He's got so much to prove, and not just on the pitch – so why aren't his mum, teachers and best mate on his side?

Jamie Johnson can't believe his luck. He's playing for Kingfield School in a Cup semi-final and scouts from his favourite club, Hawkstone United, are coming to watch!

But Jamie's hopes of a professional career still have a long way to go…

There's a huge buzz around Jamie Johnson. He's being talked about as one of the country's most talented young players. But just when he's set for stardom, a shocking event threatens to end his career for ever.

Can Jamie cope with his toughest challenge yet?

"World class – genuine world class – that's for ever. Now, the question is: are YOU world class?"

It's the big one! At last, the World Cup beckons for Jamie Johnson. It's the defining moment of his career. But which country will he play for? And will his special skills match up against the greatest players on earth?

This was the team of teams. The club of clubs. And now they wanted him to join them. A transfer to the best club in the world beckons for Jamie Johnson. This is big. This is huge!

However, a time bomb is already ticking within Jamie. . . Is the final whistle about to blow?